RESURRECTION

HARALD LUTZ BRUCKNER

For Doris

Books by Harald Lutz Bruckner

The Blue Sapphire Amulet

The Birken Saga
A Trilogy

Book 1: *Escape on the Astral Express*
Book 2: *A Wanderer on the Earth*
Book 3: *The Born-Again Phoenix*

Harald's Garland

Lighthouse Mystery

Doretta's Damnation

A Backward Glance at Eden

Obsessive Compulsion

Forever Greta

Chapter 1

URGENT! Urgent! Urgent! Red and blue neon lights flashed on and off in front of his eyes. A shadowy figure scurried down foggy lanes of the *Altstadt* in Düsseldorf. Badly stained cheap paper beer coasters, carrying smudged messages, floated down gutters driven by the steady wind rising off the river. The elegant city on the Rhein lay deep in slumber. Empty streets stared at him in silence. A drunkard spilled his guts on the sidewalk. Whoever he was, he didn't walk; the man ran. An inner voice drove him on. His emotions were in overdrive, drowning him in fear, anger, sadness, and frustration. His dream had become a nightmare.

When Lenny Osram finally awoke his pajama top was damp with sweat. He stared at the earthlike mobile hanging above his bed. He was mesmerized by the long, skinny country straddling the Pacific side of the South American continent. *I can't get those fellows out of my head. My God, could it be them? That resemblance was shocking.* Lenny took a deep breath. He searched for his iPhone wanting to share his discovery with his twin brother. *Perhaps it isn't a case of discovery at all.* But no matter how hard he tried to forget what he had seen, his deep suspicions wouldn't let him strike the images from his memory.

Lenny stretched his arms and legs. He scratched the gray hairs on his chest. *I hate leaving the warmth of my bed. My old bones feel so much better under the protection of down feathers.* The constant and annoying knocking on his bedroom windows had shaken him into reality. It was a hefty wind that made the barren branches of the old chestnut tree rattle against the thickly rounded windowpanes. The comfort of heated floor tiling felt good on his bare feet, but a chill in the air made him shiver. *Perhaps one of the bay windows is ajar?* Looking closer at the culprit, he peered at the grayness of the sky and was pleased it wasn't snowing or the streets glistening with freezing rain. *Wherever did I leave my slippers?*

He walked into his office. Lenny still liked the large mahogany table that had been the focal point of his workspace in years past. He glanced at the dull surface and, running his fingers across the tabletop, confirmed the need for attention. *You could stand a damn good dusting.* Ever since Anna passed away, he'd been neglectful of his home. Lenny wasn't a slob. There were no piles of dirty dishes in the kitchen sink, and bed linens didn't tell tales of sweaty nights upon awakening most mornings. He swung a vacuum cleaner on occasion; window washing, sewing, ironing, and God forbid, dusting, were clearly not his forté. Now and then the thought crossed his mind that he shouldn't be so darn frugal and engage the services of a cleaning lady.

His calendar read February 5, 2022. Lenny fumbled with his iPhone and hit the contact list, never having gotten into the habit of creating speed dial for certain people. He glared at Apple's latest version in modernity. *One of these days I'll grasp all the tricks you're trying to teach me—but not today.* He searched for his brother's new phone number. Lutz and Deborah, his wife, had moved back to Düsseldorf. Representative Dr. Lutz Osram recently retired from his government job in Berlin while the newest variant in the COVID Pandemic was still raging throughout the capital. Counting their blessings, neither Lutz nor Deborah caught the illness.

Lutz noticed the incoming call and realized it was his brother. He checked the time, giving a quick look at the display. It was just after eight o'clock. "Well, that's a nice surprise. How are you, brother? What's on your mind this chilly morning?" Lutz wished he'd stepped into his fur-lined slippers when he rushed from their bed to answer the phone. He hated having the thing resting too close to his pillow. As much as he liked technology, the ease of invading people's privacy had become a bone of contention.

"I rarely pay attention to commercials on the radio. Earlier, I looked at the paper and saw an ad for Schumacher's *Im Goldenen Kessel* and remembered the great time we had at the place when we celebrated our eightieth birthday," Lenny said.

"You did have to remind me. My God, we're getting to be ancient!" A noisy yawn punctuated his exclamation. "You mean to say that's the reason for getting me out of bed at this hour?" Lutz knew he needed to interrupt the flow of verbiage. Under certain circumstances, Lenny was known to have a gift for gab.

There was a lengthy pause. Lenny was stalling for time. He wasn't quite certain how to approach his brother with his cockamamie brainstorm, still blabbering about that long-ago eightieth birthday party. "I dislike being alone on such occasions. I still miss Anna; she remained my soulmate until the moment she died." He hesitated before he spoke again and didn't know what made him say what he said next. "It's really too bad neither of us had any kids. I'm thinking of our sister; she had four." Lenny coughed and cleared his throat. His voice sounded raspy.

Lutz expressed concern. "Are you feeling okay?"

"I'm just dandy. Don't mind my little cough. I'm not suffering with the Corona/Covid virus—the topic and convenient excuse for anything that might go wrong on a given day."

"Strange, you of all people, reminding me of our childless existence. Deborah still thinks we should have tried harder after she and I finally got married. But tell me what really prompted you to call? Certainly not to talk about children, their absence in our lives, or our long-forgotten 80th birthday? Deb and I wondered why we hadn't heard from you since we've been back in town for a while. You haven't been sick, have you?"

"No, not at all. I told you I'm fine. I'm too mean to give up. Weeds don't die. On the other hand, my phone also rings. Joking. I've been busy going through old stuff and deciding what to ditch, what to digitize, and what to keep just the way it is. I'm not even sure I ought to bring up my actual reason for uncluttering my office." Lenny looked at his raggedy fingernails. *You could stand a good trimming.*

Lutz couldn't imagine what prompted his brother's activities, curiosity in his voice. "Oh, you're finally seeing the light? Getting rid of all that old stuff you hang onto is good! Who will care after you are gone?" Lutz pictured what Lenny's office looked like.

Lenny hesitated again. "You're absolutely correct. But what made me think about old photo albums was a strange discovery I made a couple of days ago when I went into the *Altstadt* and enjoyed a stein or two sitting at the bar of the old haunt."

"What was that? You mean at the *Goldenen Kessel?*"

Lutz was tempted to reach for his pipe, knowing he was in for a lengthy revelation. Lenny knew how to chew off one's ear. He never completely forgot that car-salesmen spiel after he finally retired and sold the business. In years past, once Lenny had someone's attention, they never drove off the lot without a new Bugatti or Bentley.

"Come on. Spit it out!" Lutz demanded.

"There were these two fellows that caught my eye. I swear they looked like they could've been your or my sons. The resemblance was uncanny," Lenny spoke with some hesitation in his utterance.

"What got you so shook up? I had a hard time following what you were saying." Lutz's eyes had popped wide open. *I knew there was an ulterior motive for this early-morning call.*

Slow down, Lenny, slow down! Lenny admonished himself. "I could shoot myself for not having the guts to approach them. When they got up and left, I asked the bartender if they were regulars. He told me he'd seen them a few times before. He wasn't sure if he'd call them regulars," Lenny went on.

"Yeah, probably as regular as you and I have been in that place. How old were they?" Lutz inquired.

Lenny frowned for a second. "I guess somewhere in their fifties; maybe at best very late forties. Honest to God, they looked like us in the prime of our lives!"

Lutz was puzzled. Too many questions instantly crossed that legal mind of his. "My God, Lenny. You can't be serious? You're not thinking of Doretta's stolen twins? They disappeared more than fifty years ago. And not in Düsseldorf but at the outskirts of Santiago, Chile. Just the thought of it blows me away." Lutz wished Deborah would hand him his first cup of coffee. He needed to be fully engaged for what Lenny had to say.

"Stranger things than that have happened. Of course, the two men didn't sound Spanish. Neither did they strike me as truly native. While they were conversing in fluent German with the bartender, I detected some kind of Slavic undertones. I'm still pissed at myself for letting them get away. I just sat there, stared at them, and peeked over my half-empty stein like a mouse searching for an escape route while glaring at the steely eyes of Tom the cat. Lutz, I swear, I thought I was looking at us when we were that age."

"I'm getting what you're saying. This is beginning to sound morbid but interesting," Lutz mumbled.

"How would you and Deborah feel about joining me tomorrow night for dinner at the *Kessel?* We ought to celebrate our eighty-eighth. For once, just humor me. Perhaps we'll be lucky enough and run into those chaps. Who knows? I've always been a great believer in serendipity." Lenny took a last sip from his mug of Irish coffee. The Keurig had done a great job. *Just what I needed to start the day.*

Lutz mulled over the idea. "You are in luck that this birthday falls on a Sunday. I wouldn't do it if the celebration involved a Friday night or a Saturday before sunset. I know it's not your thing, but I refuse to let anything interfere with *Shabbat* and temple," Lutz said. "What time did you have in mind?" He asked, quickly checking his calendar.

"How about six o'clock? Are you still driving? I'll grab a cab. That way I won't have to worry about having a drink," Lenny offered.

"No problem. I still enjoy my independence and drive whenever I can. I have no issue with non-alcoholic beverages. In a pinch, club soda will do. I've gotten to like it with a twist of lemon. Of course, these days most breweries offer great-tasting nonalcoholic beer. It's an acquired taste," Lutz said.

"I ought to try that sometime. They probably offer it in a bottle at the *Kessel.* I just like and prefer a tap beer," Lenny said.

"Anyway, we'll see you tomorrow night. Thanks for the suggestion. You're right; we should celebrate this birthday after all we've been through in the last year or so. We need to forget 2020 and 2021. At the rate we're going, 2022 will be forgettable too."

"Right! Give a hug to Deborah." Lenny touched the off button. He decided to ditch the robe and crawled back into bed. He shivered for a moment and was thankful that the down of the *Federbett* [duvet] still held the warmth of his body. "On mornings like this I really miss having a warm body next to me," he mumbled. Only lately he noticed talking to himself or the radio.

"Will do!" Lutz said, suddenly realizing that Lenny had ended the call unceremoniously. *Mein Gott! Could those two really be Elijah Avraham and Eduardo Emmanuel Garcia López?* His brow resembled Grandma's old wooden washboard. Countless questions crossed his mind as he sat down with Deborah who enjoyed her second cup of coffee.

"That was Lenny as you could guess. He insists we join him for dinner at *Im Goldenen Kessel* tomorrow night. Guess he wants to make up for lost time. It's been eight years since we celebrated our birthday together. I believe he's right. At our age, we shouldn't pass up such an opportunity."

Deborah reached for the coffee urn, poured Lutz a cup, and placed the tray with sugar and cream in front of him. "I agree. We shouldn't. I couldn't help catching part of the conversation. What was that all about?" She drew the softness of a Merino wool blanket across her shoulders. The warmth of the fading fire in the *Kamin* [open fireplace] gave up competing with the cold of the early morning passing through large plate glass windows.

"I'll spare you the details. You know Lenny. I often think he should never have sold his business when he did. Making a killing selling fancy cars was the source of his happiness."

"But that conversation had nothing to do with the sale of cars."

"Don't be so impatient." He took a first sip of his coffee. "He spotted a couple of men at the *Kessel* that reminded him of himself and me in our younger years. Believe it or not, he thinks they could be my long-lost sister's twins who were abducted all those many years ago." He read the shock in Deborah's eyes.

"Your memory is often much better than mine. You met the boys' distraught mother when she came to be with Mom after my stepfather died on the plane moments before they landed in Düsseldorf. You didn't forget?" Lutz asked.

"How could I? Your parents, Gisela and Andreas, were on their way back from Santiago having made that long trip to console Doretta and her family. It was all so sad," Deborah responded.

"Lenny is talking about Elijah Avraham and Eduardo Emmanuel who were taken from their home while Doretta and Fernando and the older kids were on that trip to Antarctica." He kept shaking his head. "Who wouldn't have been distraught?" Lutz never forgot the sadness he'd seen in his sister's eyes.

Deborah saw him pressing the knuckles of his index fingers into the sockets of his eyes. "Wouldn't it be something if Lenny's right in his crazy speculation? What *would* you do?" she asked.

"First we'll have to meet those two gentlemen and talk. I would have to see a lot more than a strong resemblance. It does happen sometimes among total strangers. And if they are indeed who Lenny suspects they are, then we'll be looking at a puzzle with at least a thousand pieces. Let's be honest, what is the possibility of these two men being our nephews? That happened fifty-some years ago in another hemisphere."

Deborah took a sip from her coffee cup. "That's a long time, indeed."

"I can't even recall what those kids looked like, never mind speculate whom they might resemble today. For all intents and purposes, they might have been killed just like the rest of Doretta's family. I just don't know where to begin with that thought process. Guess I can't jump over that conservative shadow of mine."

"But that was just it. There never was any evidence that those boys were murdered. They simply vanished from the face of the earth. I recall Doretta telling us that the police used dogs, even their own dog. They had access to scents of the boys, and still, they never turned up a trace of those kids. And then Doretta and the entire family disappeared in 1973. It was all so weird."

"All we ever knew was from that German lady in Santiago who wrote to Mother about what she had learned from the servant who had worked on the hacienda for many years. I remember Mother being shocked when she heard what they had done to Esmeralda, the boys' Chilean grandmother," Lutz recalled.

Deborah hung on every word Lutz said. Her imagination ran wild. She could still clearly see Doretta's face when she spoke of the boys' disappearance, hoping they weren't hurt or abused but delivered into loving hands. Deborah smiled at Lutz. "Now I *am* intrigued," she sighed as she took Lutz's hand and steered him in the direction of their bedroom.

"Let's take a hot shower and clear our heads," Lutz said over his shoulder. "We really need to think this one through and through." He tried to envision a picture of himself at age fifty.

Chapter 2

LENNY climbed out of his rumpled bed after a restless night. He peered out the window. Looking up at the sky, darkness stared back at him. The curvature of the bent-glass windows dimmed the distant street lights. *Who cares? I'm not disturbing anyone.* He kept thinking about the discovery he shared with his brother the day before. *I'm so glad I'm like Grandma. She never threw anything away. I know I kept all the letters Doretta sent. No way did I dispose of the wonderful slides she mailed. I just have to remember where I stored all that stuff.*

Still in his striped silk pajamas, he walked toward the office. *Nice way to start the day on my eighty-eighth birthday,* he thought.

Of course, the logical place to start looking was his office, although none of those things would be stored in the metal file cabinets where he kept all business records. Lenny turned to the solid walnut cabinet and slid back one of the louvered doors.

Row after row of photo albums met his eyes. *I know she hardly ever sent prints; Fernando liked working with slides, that much I do remember. Later, Mario, the older boy, took lots of photos, too. Always slides, like father, like son.* Lenny thought back to the time when he helped his mother with the purchase of the fancy Leica she wanted to give her first grandson.

He closed that door and moved to the right. When he opened the next louver, he faced a ton of slide trays, all neatly labeled according to content and dates. How well he recalled the years before digital photography obsoleted film. *Modern photography is a blessing,* he thought.

"Wow!" He couldn't believe how many slides he'd amassed in all those years. His search carried him through the neat stacks of boxes. He spotted "1968." Lenny pushed his new trifocals into a better position on his nose allowing him to read the small writing. And there it was, the tray he was searching for. "The birth of Elijah Avraham and Eduardo Emmanuel—Christmas 1968."

His hands were trembling as he held the slide tray. *Now what did I do with that old projector? Haven't used it in years. I know I didn't get rid of it. But where the heck is it? Never mind that old thing. What about the lighted sorting box I used to have?* He realized he was getting too impatient. *Forget it!* He lifted the slightly dusty cover off the box and set it on his desk. He took out one slide after another. Lenny held each up to a light bulb until he ran across one that made his heart skip a beat. He was looking at closeups taken of the boys the day they were born.

Suddenly he remembered inheriting all the correspondence his grandmother had with Doretta. Once again he was thankful, Grandma had been a hoarder and never disposed of anything written to her. He rummaged through the wooden box that once kept a tree cake. *Mother sent it to Grandma for Christmas. How I loved watching the neighborhood baker pouring the dough onto the rotating spindle. Each layer of dough browned before spreading the next and thus creating the look of tree rings.*

Such wonderful memories. At the time of her passing, he had chosen to keep what Grandma had stored in that old box, all those treasured notes she received through the years from special people. Doretta's letters were among them. He ran his hand across the many pieces of vital information, lovingly tucked back into their envelopes and bundles held together by pink silk ribbons. He cast a look toward the framed photo of his grandmother. It was standing under the lamp on his desk. A tear ran down his right cheek. He drew in the air and thought he could smell her perfume.

He turned his attention back to the wooden box. Of course, the letters were arranged in order according to dates when they were written. It took only minutes before he found the one Doretta wrote to her grandmother the day Elijah Avraham and Eduardo Emmanuel were born. He remembered Grandma expressing her feelings about the choice of such Jewish-sounding middle names. It was Lutz who recognized the reason for Doretta's plan. He knew she did it to honor their father.

Lenny read the letter out loud. What caught his attention was the comment that the boys were identical in looks with the exception of a tiny white birthmark resembling the shape of an anchor on Elijah's left cheek. Doretta wrote that she thought the twins favored the Osram linage. *How perceptive!*

If it was a birthmark indeed, it wouldn't have disappeared. Of course, worse, he might have had it surgically removed. He rubbed his itchy nose before he put his glasses back on. *You're letting yourself get carried away far too much. Just forget about it.* But he couldn't just forget about it. Lenny picked up his phone. It was ten o'clock. He saw no problem giving Lutz a quick call.

Lutz glanced at the phone and spoke. "This is getting to be a habit. What's up now, dear brother"

"Happy birthday!" Lenny said.

"Well, the same to you. What's so urgent this early in the day?"

"I got up hours ago and searched through my treasure trove in the old office. I haven't even scratched the surface as far as slides and letters are concerned."

"So, what did you unearth?"

"I read the letter our sister wrote to Grandma the day those boys were born. She talks about Elijah Avraham, the first-born, having a distinguishing white birthmark on his left cheek. That might be our first clue if those two should surface again. I still cannot believe I let them get away without having spoken when I first spotted them."

"Don't be so damn hard on yourself. I can see that happening to me, although my legal mind is already turning over leaf after leaf in this unfolding story of intrigue."

"So what should be our next move?" Lenny asked.

"Let's just see if they make an encore appearance, giving us the opportunity to make great discoveries. Don't forget those boys were barely three years old when they disappeared. How much do you remember of what happened in 1937?" Lutz asked.

"I remember Father and Grandma. I liked the sound of our father's gentle voice. Grandma always wore that horrible perfume. Of course, she was around for many more years, allowing that memory to be reinforced." Lenny took a deep breath.

"Are you feeling okay?" Lutz interrupted.

"I watched from my bedroom window when the Nazis came and took Dad. I'm glad I had turned away and didn't see them beat him half to death. Doretta saw the whole thing and had nightmares for many years whenever she relived the events of that day. She was eleven when that took place," Lenny responded. There were tears in his eyes.

"I know, I know. And we were both only nine when they took Dad away. It's amazing what we seem to recall," Lutz said.

"But what do you remember from the days when you were much younger?" Lenny asked.

"My earliest memories take me back to when we were around

three. I can remember Dad's dark and very sad eyes and I agree his voice seemed quite different. When he hugged us before he left for the day, I was always aware of the aftershave lotion he wore," Lutz said.

"What was it? Old Spice?" Lenny joked.

"Maybe! I don't recall many details of the place where we lived. It was an older house, and we lived on the second floor. Dad must have practiced law somewhere away from home. I'm sure, we didn't have a car and often rode streetcars and buses to visit Grandma. I suppose I might remember more with the help of old photos," Lutz posed.

"That's what I'm thinking, too. Pictures might stir up old memories. But let's not get ahead of ourselves and too far off the mark. First, we must see those fellows again and play it carefully before we jump in with both feet," Lenny said. While he was speaking with Lutz, he held some more of the old slides up to the light. His busy mind kept telling him to keep searching.

For a moment Lutz thought he might have become disconnected. "Are you still there?" he asked. "I won't keep you. Deb and I are looking forward to seeing you tonight at the *Kessel*. We'll have plenty of time to chat about this."

"I'll call a little later and ask for a table with a good view of the entrance as well as the bar. Just playing it safe. If the same bartender is on duty tonight, we might want to give him our business cards. Perhaps he will consider giving us a jingle should those gentlemen turn up another night. Greasing his palms a bit might be beneficial, too," Lenny said.

"Good plan! Keep digging. Until later." Lutz smiled to himself as he touched the red button on his trusted phone. Lenny was in his all-business mode, ready to clinch the deal; for Lutz it was all about legal implications. He couldn't wait to learn more. The phrase "what if" crossed his mind!

Chapter 3

Lutz and Deborah walked into the *Goldenen Kessel* shortly after six. Their eyes adjusted to the candle-lit scene. Lutz glanced up at the wooden beams and the smoke-stained ceiling. An enticing mix of odors from burning candles, beer, and *Sauerbraten* hung in the air. They saw Lenny protecting a desirable location. When he spotted them, he rose from his chair to assist Deborah with getting seated at the table.

"Glad you made it." Lenny hugged Deborah. She wished him only the best on his birthday. He reached to shake hands with his brother but Lutz felt he needed to hug, too. "It's been too long. I've missed seeing you," Lutz put his arms around his brother and then stepped back.

"You're pretty lean; still running when the mood strikes you?" Lenny asked.

"I don't run too often, but I work out at the gym three days a week. I do enjoy the camaraderie of my regular group," Lutz replied.

"That's good to know. I might just join you one of these mornings."

"I'll believe it when it happens," Lutz said. "If nothing else, you might enjoy the steam room. These days it's the highlight of the visit to the gym."

"You've got me almost convinced. I'll try anything that will make these old bones feel better." Lenny raised his arms over his head and gave them a quick stretch.

"I arrived here a few minutes early and got this table. It gives me a perfect view of the entrance and the bar. I see the bartender in question among the men serving tonight. Haven't had a chance to speak with him but will as soon as I notice a lull in activities," Lenny said.

"The place sure hasn't changed much. Can't believe it's eight years since Deborah and I were here last. I know what I'm having. Can't go wrong with that *Sauerbraten* and all the trimmings." He caught the attention of a *Düsseldorfer Köbess* [native waiter]. "You may start the two of us with a tall bottle of water—the "with gas" variety. My brother will have the *Schumacher Altbier*. I'm driving. Thanks." Lutz smiled and winked at the waiter.

In response, the man decked out in black and wearing a sparkling-white apron raised an eyebrow, wondering why someone would grace their pub and not have a real beer. He mumbled as he walked away from the table, "Couldn't get me to just have water."

Their drinks were served quickly, and menus were placed in their hands. Lenny couldn't help admiring the large glass with the blue writing proclaiming its content to be *Schumacher Alt*. Deborah clinked glasses with her two handsome gray-haired gentlemen. "Happy 88th birthday. I realize it's not quite kosher with soda water, but it will have to do. It's the thought that counts. I'm counting on a few more happy returns. You were blessed with your grandmother's genes." She smiled broadly.

Lenny and Lutz nodded in agreement. Grandma lived well into her 90s. While Deborah still studied the menu, Lenny decided to treat himself to a *Schweinshaxe* [roasted ham hock], knowing none were better. Deb finally settled on a *Kalbsschnitzel* [veal cutlet], being told it would be prepared to perfection by the chef.

When Deborah sought out the restroom, Lenny and Lutz took the opportunity to speak with the bartender. They read his name tag, discovering they were dealing with Hans Lang. Lenny got his attention, tapping the wooden bar. "Herr Lang, I spoke to you a few days ago about a couple of chaps sitting at the bar. Have you seen them since that day? By the way, I'm Lenny Osram. Meet my brother Lutz."

The men shook hands.

"Make it Hans. They were here last night. Sat at the bar for quite a while and spoke in some strange language, although they addressed me in perfect German. Sometimes I thought they sounded like Russians. I'm not really all that good with foreign languages. Do you know what I mean? But I can pick out a local dialect."

"Got you, Hans. Too bad we didn't come last night. Would you do us a favor? Here are my brother's and my business cards with our phone numbers. Would you mind sending me a quick text next time they show? I live close by and could be here in a matter of minutes," Lenny said.

"No problem. Must be important, gentlemen! I usually don't care to become involved in personal matters with strangers," Hans commented.

Lenny slipped him a twenty-Euro bill. "It's critical to both of us. We are just on a fishing expedition; those two gentlemen might have a connection to our family."

Hans looked puzzled.

"It's a long story." Lenny opted to leave it there as Deborah returned to the table.

Lutz held her chair. "Too bad we missed those two chaps. They were here last night. The bartender, Hans, is willing to contact us the next time they show. We'll just have to learn to be patient. Rome wasn't built in a day, to use a cliché."

With that, the waiter and his assistant placed their plates in front of them. They lifted the silver domes and beheld their delicious mouth-watering dinners—piping hot. They felt like *God in France.* "*Guten Appetit.* Let me know if you need anything else. Another *Altbier*, sir?" the waiter asked Lenny.

"Why not? I'll grab a cab. No problem. Thank you for being so attentive," Lenny said.

He was pleased Lutz and Deborah were willing to join him for dinner and chat about their time in Berlin. It was a welcome distraction from the fact that he had missed the chance to speak with the intriguing strangers.

Deborah crossed her knife and fork, taking a pause. "We really treasured our days in Berlin. I loved having three opera houses in the same city. The shopping was wonderful. While Lutz busied himself politicking at the *Reichstag* [German Capitol], I enjoyed playing the eternal tourist. There's so much history. We made it out to Potsdam a few times." Deborah retrieved a small photo album from the sizable purse she carried and passed it to Lenny.

"Thought you might like to see some of these. I loved visiting Sanssouci Palace and learning all about King Frederick the Great. He was quite the enlightened ruler of Prussia. He, Voltaire, and Catherine the Great could teach today's leaders a thing or two," Deb winked at Lenny. She decided to take another bite of her delectable *Schnitzel.*

"You said it, Deb. Vladimir Putin scares the hell out of me. The recent troop buildup near Ukraine frightens me. I've never forgotten World War II. As we've often said, that display of power is too close to our borders. God help us if he goes through with his plans of conquering his neighbors. I don't know if I could face another disaster. The Pandemic was devastating enough. There were days when I questioned the wisdom of wanting to live past my 90th birthday," Lenny said.

Lutz was glad his taste buds were still thoroughly enjoying the *Sauerbraten;* he opted not to comment. Of course, deep down he was as concerned as were Lenny and Deborah, perhaps even more so, having sat through many a discussion of what Putin's intentions might be and the implications and use of nuclear and biological warfare on the European continent—and the world for that matter.

None of them realized what would happen only eighteen days later as they hugged and kissed each other goodnight at the end of a special evening, celebrating the Osram twins' 88th birthday *Im Goldenen Kessel.* All were deep in thought as they headed for their cars.

Chapter 4

IT was February 13, shortly after 6 o'clock in the evening, when Lenny's cell vibrated with an incoming text. "The duo you're looking for just marched in and ordered. Hans."

Lenny's response was cursory. "Thanks. I'm on my way."

He called for a cab, not wishing to waste time. He arrived at *Im Goldenen Kessel* ten minutes later. Lenny spotted the two men sitting at the bar, appearing to be engaged in a serious conversation. Both were wearing fedora hats—*uncommon these days*. Europeans had become used to wearing baseball caps—even backward—the American way. As he approached the two men from behind, Lenny decided to sit next to the man on the left. Climbing onto the bar stool, he intentionally bumped into his about-to-be close neighbor at the bar. Lenny's hand flung in the air and knocked down the guy's hat. It landed at Lenny's feet.

"Sorry; I didn't mean to do that," Lenny said sheepishly. He got off the stool and retrieved the disheveled fedora, handing it back to its owner.

The guy just glared at Lenny and said something to his companion. He didn't speak German.

Lenny didn't excuse himself for sitting so close and had no intention of disclosing the reason for leaving so little space between himself and the man he was eyeing. He took a close look at the guy. *Shit! I don't remember one of them sporting a full gray beard. So much for checking out that birthmark.*

Lenny glanced at his reflection in the mirror behind the chorus of busy bartenders and an unbelievable assortment of colorful bottles. Then he studied the reflected images of the two men sitting next to him. *My God, their eyes and noses match mine. It's as if we were cloned. They must see that themselves.* Their complexion hinted at olives or honey and reflected Mediterranean heritage. He was puzzled. *How in hell am I going to approach this?*

He ordered an *Altbier.* The first sip was always the best. The rich foam clung to his upper lip and his mustache. It had been years since he'd sported a full beard. He'd shaved it off when Anna told him he should start thinking about playing Santa in front of some fancy store on the *Königsallee* [King's Boulevard]. While the strangers continued speaking softly, Lenny discerned that the men in question were conversing in some kind of Slavic dialect. He didn't think it was Russian. Lifting his glass before taking another swallow, Lenny said to the man on his right, "*Prost!* [To your health!] Where are you from?" Lenny wondered what gave him the guts to ask the question.

"What makes you ask? Is it any of your business? But since you asked so nicely, I'll tell you. We live in Düsseldorf, if that helps." He smiled broadly, knowing that gave Lenny little to go on.

Lenny got the message they were unwilling to share any more. "But that isn't your true home. Your dialect isn't that of a *Düsseldorfer Radschläger* [a native cartwheeler]. In case you don't know, boys in Düsseldorf play that trick when begging for money from unsuspecting visitors. I'm aware of these shenanigans because I spent most of my life in this city." Lenny grinned at the strangers.

"What's it to you? Can't a couple brothers just enjoy their beer and chat about what's on their minds? I'm not bothering you, am I?" He looked downright annoyed. While speaking with a distinct accent, his German utterances were grammatically flawless.

Lenny kept staring at the man's left cheek. That gray bush of a beard was simply too thick. His vision couldn't penetrate the dense growth of hair. Even if there was a birthmark, he couldn't detect it. He leaned back hoping to get a good look at the beardless man's left cheek. Unfortunately, the light wasn't good enough for him to see. Aside from that, their heads were moving targets as they engaged in their lively discussion in a language Lenny had heard in his travels across eastern Europe. It was clearly their preferred mode of communicating.

Not willing to give up so easily, Lenny ordered another beer. "Hans, why don't you freshen their drinks as well. Put it on my tab." Lenny pointed with his thumb toward the guys sitting next to him. Hans understood.

As Hans put another beer and a shot in front of the two men, the guy next to Lenny spoke.

"Дякую (Dyakuyu); that's 'thank you' in Ukrainian." He lifted his glass toward Lenny. His brother followed suit.

Lenny's immediate neighbor couldn't believe it. The shot glass slipped from his hand, the glass and its content landing in Lenny's crotch.

"Oh shit!" Lenny grabbed the empty glass before it hit the tiled floor.

"Sorry, sir. That was unintended," the bearded one said.

Hans handed Lenny a white linen napkin. "That should do it. The *Schnapps* won't stain your pants; it's pure, clear alcohol."

Lenny shrugged. He was unperturbed. "How long have you lived in Düsseldorf?" He faced his neighbor. "You didn't learn to speak German as well as you do in a few days."

"Our family fled from Yalta in 2014 when Putin made his first move to invade our country. My aunt, who raised us, spoke excellent German, and we studied the language in school. My brother and I grew up on the Crimean Peninsula. We weren't born there but that's where we lived when we were little boys."

"That's very interesting. You must be glad to have come here when you did. What kind of work were you able to find after you arrived in Germany?" Lenny asked.

"Both my brother and I and a close friend of ours studied at the Crimean Humanitarian University in Yalta." He pointed at his brother. "He became a professor of Psychiatry and eventually taught at the Mechnikov National University in Odessa."

"That's interesting. So both of you decided on a life in academia?" Lenny interjected.

"Yes. My graduate studies leading to a PhD in modern languages I did at the Taras Shevchenko National University of Kyiv. I returned to Yalta wanting to be closer to home."

"Wouldn't Kyiv have been a more exciting place to live?"

"Yes and no. I didn't feel I could leave my aunt to fend for herself. So I taught at the Crimean University until we escaped just in time. Now we are worried about distant relations still living in Ukraine. We haven't seen any of them in eight years," the bearded man said.

Lenny was spellbound. "My name is Leonard Osram. It used to be Osramski. My father was an Ashkenazi Jew. His ancestors emigrated from Odessa generations ago. I've never been called anything but Lenny."

"I'm Maksym Popov. This guy here is my twin, Matviyko." He laid a hand on his brother's shoulder. Matviyko responded, waving his shot glass in Lenny's direction. "Supposedly he was born a few minutes later than I. I have no idea where Aunt Sofia learned that little tidbit, but that was what she used to tell us. I suppose she invented the story that I'm the greatest, and Matviyko is said to be God's gift. So she always treated us according to the meanings of our names."

Maksym stared at Lenny. He saw the tears in the man's eyes. He laid his left hand on Lenny's shoulder. Lenny remembered his grandmother telling such stories. Although she was dead and buried for many years, both he and Lutz venerated their grandmother and cherished their memories.

"Sorry! You've got to forgive a sentimental old man. Those revelations of yours touched me. It sounds so terribly sad. I'm glad you made it to Düsseldorf and that you are safe. Is your Aunt Sofia still living?" Lenny inquired. What he longed to do was to embrace the stranger. It was a feeling deep in his soul that kept nagging him. It was as if Doretta was reaching out from the grave, asking in her beautiful voice to rediscover and love her lost boys. He looked at Maksym, searching for answers in the stranger's eyes.

Maksym, aware of a certain undercurrent, was tempted to reach out to Lenny. "Aunt Sofia is very much alive. We celebrated her 85th birthday just a few days ago. She's adjusted well to living here and spends time with our families and us on holidays and special occasions. Two years ago, we finally convinced her to move into a senior center in Kaiserswerth."

"That's a nice town. Many seniors spend their golden years there," Lenny said.

"Yes. It's a pleasant place and she seems to enjoy her days. Needless to say, transplanting someone to a new world at age seventy-seven wasn't easy. But she wouldn't have it any other way. All she had was us, and she would never have considered staying behind in

Yalta. But let me not bore you with our tales of woe. You didn't come here for that."

"No, no. That's where you're mistaken. I love hearing about your journey, especially under the circumstances. How often does one meet persons at an old bar in the *Altstadt* of Düsseldorf who came here from Yalta?" He kept studying Maksym's face. *Who knows how you wound up in Yalta? We may never find the answer,* thought Lenny.

"Both Matviyko and I have held positions at the Heinrich Heine University since 2016. The gods were kind to us when they made it possible for us to find decent work as displaced persons."

"I'm pleased to learn that you found fitting employment in the new Vaterland," Lenny said.

"Matviyko is a confirmed bachelor but has a significant other. I married my wife, Daryna, in 1993. Our daughter, Nataliya, just graduated from the university with her doctorate in Economics. She married Anton Hugenpott, one of her professors, and is about to make us grandparents for the first time. Going on fifty-four, I never thought that would happen."

"Wow! That's wonderful. Congratulations! I'm so pleased I had this chance to talk with you. I have a twin brother as well. His name is Lutz. In some ways, we're like you. I never married and my significant other passed away not too long ago. Lutz was smart enough to marry, but unfortunately neither of us had children." Lenny took another sip from his beer.

Maksym felt as if Lenny's eyes bored right through him.

"Since we have this long-distance connection to Odessa, Lutz would probably enjoy meeting you. He's particularly fond of that city and his Jewish heritage. Lutz practices his faith. I'm supposed to be Catholic but don't attend any churches. Somehow, organized religion never did anything for me. Perhaps it has something to do with what happened to my father," Lenny continued.

Maksym gawped at him as Lenny continued speaking. "Why don't I give you my business card. Let's stay in touch. I'd love to get to know you better," Lenny said.

"Thank you, Lenny, if I may call you that?" He glanced at the card. "That's thoughtful of you. I've never met anyone in a bar where I felt an almost instant connection. Matviyko and I will make a point of contacting you." Maksym extended his hand to Lenny and wished him a good evening. He couldn't help himself; there was something about the old man nagging for his attention.

Maksym had been looking at his watch a few times too often. He knew his wife must be wondering why he was gone for such a long time. "We better head home," he said to Matviyko.

Lenny raised his right hand, giving Hans the money sign, suggesting he'd like to have the bill.

Hans reached for the *Bierdeckel,* adding quickly all the scratch marks for the drinks the three men had consumed during the evening.

Lenny handed him forty-five Euro and called it even. "Thanks, Hans, for your excellent service." He winked at the bartender.

They got off the bar stools and turned toward the heavy oak doors, shielded by a leather windbreak. Lenny walked out of the *Kessel* flanked by the strangers. The twins from Yalta had failed to comprehend the deep sadness reflected in his eyes. All he could think about was that they might indeed be his sister's twins who vanished from their home on the outskirts of Santiago, Chile, fifty-one years earlier. Tears were once again running down his cheeks as he flagged a cab. Doretta's image flashed in front of his eyes. *How could we ever lose sight of you? What happened to you and your loved ones? Who would do such a thing?* Lenny's mind was in a whirl.

He entered the cab without saying a word. The driver kept staring at him and asked where he wished to go. Lenny gave his address to the cabby, speaking in a broken voice.

He got out of the car and paid the man, almost making the mistake of handing the cabby a fifty instead of a twenty-Euro bill. He grasped the handrail as he attempted to climb the steps to the front door. There were times when he debated using a cane. *A third leg might greatly benefit me on an evening such as this. Admit it, you're becoming an old codger.*

Lenny was glad for the warmth of the house greeting him. It was the stillness of the place that bothered him the most. On nights like this, he missed Anna. She had been an excellent companion for so many years. He hung up his hat but simply tossed his coat on the bench gracing the foyer. For a moment he debated whether to have another drink. Then he changed his mind and headed straight for the unmade rumpled bed.

Chapter 5

Maksym waved goodbye as he saw the old man limp toward his cab without looking back. Matviyko turned to Maksym and spoke as soon as the car pulled away from the curb. "I still can't believe what just happened. How could you talk to a total stranger and provide all that personal information? He might be a spy. We both know how some of us are being monitored and watched. Of course, this guy didn't have a hint of a Russian accent. I just don't understand you though. I never thought of you as being gullible."

"I couldn't help myself. It was almost like an inner voice urged me to answer any and all of his questions. I don't know why, but I was just drawn to him. It was simply incredible how, when I looked into his eyes, I felt this strange affinity between us. Lord knows why. At times I thought I was looking at myself. Didn't you see that at all? There were moments I was tempted to ask Lenny if he was our father. I realize, of course, he's almost old enough to be our grandfather."

"Are you serious?" Matviyko blurted.

"It's been so long, I've forgotten what Dad looked like. Everyone in our family vanished overnight, and I've never again seen a trace of any of our loved ones. I vaguely remember Mom and our much older brother and sister. Can you recall their names? I think it was Grandma who told us they were all killed in a plane crash," Maksym said.

"You're utterly confused. Don't you remember anything that happened?" Matviyko's face appeared flushed. He wanted to shake his brother into reality, or better yet, confront him with a different reality than the one Maksym experienced in his night terrors. "You are confusing what Aunt Sofia told us she learned from the stranger who dumped us at her home. I don't remember any grandmother. There was just Aunt Sofia and her tales of woe," Matviyko said. He was furious with himself, remembering even less of the distant past than Maksym. Yet, he was thankful never to have lived through the shocking nocturnal wanderings Maksym had experienced through the years.

Maksym unbuttoned his coat. "I need to feel the coolness of the night. I'm having hot flashes like a woman in menopause. Actually, I'm sweating like a hog. I hope this evening doesn't take me back again to those days nearly fifty years ago. Those nightmares are horrible," he said.

Matviyko put an arm around his brother. "I'm hopeful that won't happen. I've never figured out why I remained so unaffected."

Maksym's eyes brimmed with tears as he faced Matviyko. "I've got to get home. Daryna is probably wondering what happened to me. She knew we were having a drink but not a lengthy discussion and a meeting with a total stranger."

Maksym raised his arm to flag a cab. "We'd better not drive with as much as we drank. Let's grab a cab. Our cars will be good overnight in the parking lot." Stumbling, he grabbed the lapels of Matviyko's fur-lined coat collar to keep himself from falling.

"Steady boy! Steady. For once, you're making good sense. Neither you nor I can afford to land in jail on DUI charges," Matviyko pointed out.

The two men held onto each other. Neither could've walked a straight line. They were thankful for the dry pavement and that the weatherman's predictions of freezing rain had not come true.

X

Daryna had been watching the disturbing evening news while folding clothes just out of the dryer and still warm. She peeked out from her living room window when the car approached their home shortly before nine o'clock. She turned off the TV as soon as she heard the slam of the cab door. Her husband was gone for longer than three hours, supposedly just having a friendly drink with his brother. She saw Maksym stumble as he emerged from the vehicle and realized he'd lifted one too many. Daryna was thankful that he'd been smart enough not to drive.

She greeted Maksym with a not-so-convincing smile. "Were you discussing current happenings with your dear brother? It's only lately that I've noticed this side of you. You never used to have more than one beer. What's bugging you? Are you worried about what's going on? For now we are all safe here, and you have a secure position. The days of worrying lie far behind us." She laid a hand on his shoulder since he appeared to be unsteady on his feet.

"It has nothing to do with what's happening in Ukraine. I don't want to talk about it right now."

She couldn't recall Maksym ever being curt with her.

"All I'm interested in is my bed and a good night's sleep." *What a joke,* he laughed out loud. He ignored her helping hand and barely made his way to their bedroom. He tossed his fedora and smiled, a silly expression on his face, when the hat landed perfectly on top of a coat rack standing in the corner close to their bed. Next, he kicked off his loafers and then removed his pullover with a jerky motion. His suspenders slipped off his shoulders, and the creased pants dropped to the floor. Maksym gave them a swift kick before he stripped down to his underwear. He didn't even bother to remove his socks before he fell into bed and was sound asleep by the time Daryna covered him with the comforts of a *Federbett*.

When she turned down her nightlight, she could hear his heavy breathing and felt him tossing and turning but decided not to waken him. Her mind was preoccupied with the events in Ukraine. Having quickly surrendered to sleep herself, she never heard Maksym's strained voice as if begging for help.

※

Had Daryna listened to Maksym, she would have said his babble sounded almost like that of a very young child, a jumble of languages and words. What Maksym actually experienced in his subconscious state was a replay of a scene when he spoke for the last time with his father.

"Hola Papa! Are you having a good time? Eduardo and me miss you. When's you coming home?"

"Hola Elijah! We had a great time at this park. Some day you will do this with your brothers and me. Mommy and Alona had fun too, but Mario and I really enjoyed the hikes at Torres del Paine."

"What that, Papa?"

"I'll show you when I'm back. Is your brother there?"

"Si Papa, here he is. You have fun with the penguins. Take lots of pictures. Miss you, Papa. I love you."

"I love you too, Elijah!"

Eduardo grabbed the phone. "Hola Papa! I hear you have lots of fun with our brother. Is he good boy like us? You see any penguins?"

"Hola Eduardo! Mario is a very good boy. No, we've not seen any penguins so far. That comes next. I promise I will take lots of pictures. Are you behaving yourselves and not making trouble for Juanita and Grandma Esmeralda?"

"Si Papa, Elijah and me very good boys. We play lot in yard. Me, Pablo, and Elijah like new hiding places in thing you built. Me forget name you call it. He likes running in it. Pablo better than Elijah and me finding his way back home."

"You be careful in the labyrinth. Papa didn't want you to explore the maze by yourselves. You and Elijah stay out of it until I'm there. We'll do it together. Do you understand me?"

"Si Papa. Me good boy. Grandma wants to talk. Adiós Papa. Te amo, Papa."

"I love you too, Eduardo!"

𐤟

Maksym could hardly breathe as he awoke from the dream. It was always so real. The sheet under him was soaked in sweat. He ran his right hand across his hairy damp chest. Just for a moment he thought he might have wet the bed. He stared at the ceiling. He'd spoken Spanish and listened to the voice of his father who spoke about his brother and sister. *Who is Elijah and the boy called Eduardo? Where was the thing called a labyrinth of which father spoke? Who are Juanita and Grandma Esmeralda?* He squeezed his eyes shut, hoping his mind would take him back just one more time to the place where he'd just been in this frequently recurring dream. *My God! It's not a dream. It's a nightmare! Why can't I travel back in time?*

That scene was challenging enough. He longed for sleep. It didn't come easy. He recited without voicing the labels from years past, starting with 2022, counting backward in Ukrainian. Succumbed to exhaustion, his mind drifted off into sleep, only to face further darkness as his mind searched for answers. His nocturnal adventures unfolded like film noir, frightening nightmares he'd rather forget. No matter how often he experienced them, they haunted him for days without ever opening doors to the past.

Maksym felt as if he were reading a bad movie script. There is this woman. She speaks only Spanish. Her name is Juanita. Her dark eyes smile at me lovingly. Her name is strange, but I'm sure that's what others called her. She's gone into the house to fetch lunch. My brother and I hear someone stumbling out of the maze. I see it all now. I almost stop breathing not recognizing the shadowy figure. A strange man, a very big man who faces my brother and me. We are looking at a real giant. Before we know it, he's covered our mouths with some sticky gray tape and tossed both of us into a huge black sack. Within seconds we are riding in an automobile that rushes away at great speed. The tires are squealing. I smell the burning rubber.

We know we're in deep trouble when we find ourselves with strange-sounding people on a small plane. Once we are airborne, the dark man pulls off the tape he'd put on our mouths. He is merciless. We scream. Our faces hurt where he removed the sticky tape. We want our papa and mama. "Stop your crying." He pushes me hard into the seat. "No one can help you. I took care of Daddy, your mom and those other brats," he laughs satanically. I see golden teeth way back in his throat. "Your father's plane went up in smoke. They are all kaput and down in the ocean. I got you now, and I won't let you go. You boys are going for a long ride. You're my meal ticket." He laughs again, flashing his nicotine-stained front teeth. I cannot see his eyes. They are hiding behind very dark glasses. But he is big.

After a while, the plane seems to rush toward the ground. We think we're going to crash. We cry out loud. He slaps us hard. I bleed from my nose. Once the small plane lands, we're taken by the big man to a much larger airplane. It isn't long, and we're flying again, this time much higher. I have to pee and ask where I can go. The mean man pulls me by one of my ears and takes me to the bathroom. "Take a piss and make it quick," he hollers. His Spanish sounds weird. His accent is strange. I don't know who he is.

It's not long, and darkness is all around us. They feed us some sour-tasting soup that seems to be purple in color. The bread tastes awful but we don't complain. My brother and I finally fall asleep. We are still way above a large body of water when the sun comes up. Hours later the plane once again turns sharply toward the ground. We scream in fear. When we emerge, we're surrounded by people we neither know nor understand. We have no idea where we are. We start to cry. The giant slaps us hard. Once again, we're thrown into a big black bag and taken away on a wild ride. Whatever they say is like gibberish.

When they spring us from the smelly black bag, we're facing a younger woman, perhaps in her thirties. Her hair is blondish, in braids that are arranged like a crown on her head. She looks at us with a big smile. There's something almost angelic about her. Her cheeks are the color and softness of ripe peaches. Her eyes sparkle. She tries speaking to us. The mean giant treats her badly. He is rough when he grabs her arm. She tries to pull away but can't. He screams at her in a language we don't understand.

Maksym turned on his back. He had been totally lost in his nocturnal travels through scenes that replayed deep in his subconsciousness. He was soaked to the skin. Now wide awake, he recalls the tale shared by the kind woman whose life they entered in such a strange way.

Aunt Sofia often recounted what happened. She always cried when she took us back to the day the Giant Shadow dumped us into her lap. Giant Shadow is what my brother and I called the mean bastard who'd taken us. *Perhaps he stole us?* Sofia never asked us to call her Mom, and Popov never became Dad. She wanted to be called Aunt Sofia; he remained plain Popov until the day he died.

The two of them met at Livadia Palace. He was a custodian and she, being multi-lingual, a tour guide. Sofia was grace in motion; when she spoke in a lilting voice, we thought she was the sugarplum fairy. In time, we realized why the Palace officials had hired her for the job. It was her salary at the Palace that kept the ship afloat. What Popov earned paid for every bottle of booze he drank.

When she'd speak of our arrival, it was almost like a mantra deeply embedded in her mind. She'd stare into space, envisioning the giant invader: "Hand over the dough, bitch," he had yelled. "I done my job better than your old man arranged. I stole a pair of kids; you're getting two for the price of one."

Apparently Giant Shadow was curious how she and Popov learned that he was in the business of robbing South American cradles. She told him. "The word got around. Visiting the Palace, you bragged to Popov that you nabbed another kid for some barren rich bitch in town the year before. That one you stole at some favela in Rio. You were sure they'd never miss the brat. The father, a big brown dude, had assured you he was only too happy to make his wife another kid each year. They didn't know how to feed themselves, never mind more than a dozen young mouths."

"I can hear her tell that story over and over again, saying she couldn't believe what the stranger had done," Maksym mumbled.

"Aunt Sofia's words filled my head:"

'The Giant Shadow kept on spouting off about his lucrative business acumen. He told Popov he was certain he'd never be able to show his face again in Chile. When he appeared at our door, all he was interested in was the dough Popov had promised him to pay for one kid. He screamed at me to be thankful to him on bent knees. He'd risked his life to make it possible for me to finally have kids at age thirty-five.'

"Wiping her brow with a handkerchief, Aunt Sofia nodded, ready to continue her story. 'I walked out of the room and returned with a brown paper bag and glared at him. I told the Giant Shadow that I had handed him all the money Popov had. I encouraged the nasty man to leave before Popov changed his mind after awakening from his drunken stupor. I don't know what possessed me, but I whispered a thank you for making my dream of having children come true. There was no response suggesting that he understood what I tried to tell him in my broken Spanish. It always remained the language in which I was least fluent.

'I never addressed the stranger by name, because I never knew who he was. He counted the large bills contained in the bag and stuck his hoard inside the pockets of his bomber jacket. He threw the empty sack into my face,' Aunt Sofia remembered.

'The monster in our midst spoke once more.' "Hope you'll enjoy these brats. Your bastard husband paid dearly for them. Too bad the Nazis castrated him at age eighteen before the Russkis ran them out of the country." 'I made a gesture with my right hand. He gave me the finger and walked out of the house. He never gave you boys a second look.'

☰

Eventually, Aunt Sofia tried speaking to us. Her words were a mix of Spanish and some other language. We finally grasped that she tried to tell us her name. It was Sofia. When a man emerged from the bedroom, she pointed at him and kept saying "Popov." My brother and I thought that was his given name. We learned in time that we were mistaken.

Later that day we were told that our new home was called Yalta. And thus began our life in a world that was worlds apart from what we remembered.

)(

It sounded as if someone had slammed a book shut with finality. Maksym screamed for help. Daryna touched him. "Wake up, wake up. I'm here."

He turned to face his wife. Tears were running down his face. She was fully aware what had happened. It wasn't the first time in their marriage that she'd seen Maksym drift off into the distant past still desperately searching for his identity.

"You were back in Yalta during the early days, weren't you?"

"I was. It was all so vivid. Matviyko and I were threatened by the Giant Shadow and taken into a new and totally different world. Aunt Sofia was a young woman and happy to have us. We had different names. I was Elijah and Matviyko's name was Eduardo. I talked to my father on the phone and said a few words, almost speaking like a toddler. The mean stranger told us he'd killed our parents and our older brother and sister while they were traveling by plane. It was all so weird. It was all so real. I wish I could remember what they looked like. Sometimes I seem to recall their voices and certain smells."

Daryna frowned. "I wonder what brought this on? Did you talk about the early days and your strange dreams with Matviyko?"

"No. Not really. But he was there when we were approached by a complete stranger at the *Kessel* last night. I was totally taken off guard. When I looked at this old man, I thought I saw myself in the distant future. For a split second, I believed I was looking at our father. Matviyko was sure I'd lost it. Here's the guy's business card. His name is Lenny Osram. He wants to stay in touch."

Daryna held the card in her hand. She tried to make out the features of the tiny image imprinted in the upper left corner. She was tempted to look at it with a magnifying glass but refrained from getting out of bed. She hugged Maksym. "I'm so sorry seeing you so troubled. If it really bothers you, call the man and see what you can learn. What's the harm in trying? Be sure to speak to Matviyko about your dreams." She shuddered.

She got out of bed and headed for the shower. Daryna questioned whether a hot shower would change her perceptions of what she had just heard. She was well aware of her husband's difficulties dealing with the past. Whenever the subject of his origins came to the fore, he experienced his threatening encounters with incubus, the demon. Daryna often wished she could wipe the slate clean. It didn't happen. Maksym and Matviyko had to live with their troubled past. She'd often wished Maksym had taken his brother's advice to seek counseling. He refused. Unlike Matviyko, Maksym believed sharing his inner thoughts and feelings while stretched out on a stranger's couch was unmanly. *What a foolish perception for a man as educated as Maksym.*

Chapter 6

Lutz touched the accept button when he saw who tried to reach him. Deborah was in the shower. It was hair-washing day, and she'd be a good while luxuriating under the spell of warm water. He was certain there wouldn't be any interruptions.

"It was too late to call you last night. I had my first encounter with the two gentlemen in question. Hans called me as soon as they showed up. I finally had enough guts to approach them at the bar. I learned a lot."

"Like what?"

"Their names are Maksym and Matviyko Popov, and they moved to Düsseldorf from Yalta in 2014."

"You're joking. From Yalta? No wonder Hans thought they sounded Russian."

"They and an old aunt fled the Crimean Peninsula when Putin invaded their country. They are both professional men teaching at Heinrich Heine University for the last six years. Maksym is married and has a daughter who's about to present them with their first grandchild. Matviyko thinks the way I do; he never got married. I don't know if it's of any importance, but Matviyko is a practicing psychiatrist.   "This is beginning to sound more interesting all the time. Do you want to see when they can get together with us? I'm hesitant to invite total strangers into our home. We don't know much about those two, but I have no problem chatting at some bar. What do you say?"

"I'll call Maksym. If he's teaching, his wife can take a message. I had the impression they all speak pretty good German. As soon as I know something more concrete, I'll call you," Lenny said.

Lutz touched the red button. *Boy, now he's got me thinking.*

〤

Daryna heard the ring and answered the phone. "Hello! Daryna Popov speaking."

"My name is Lenny Osram. May I speak with Herr Dr. Popov, please?"

"Just a moment; I'll ask him to pick up the phone."

"Thank you." Lutz thought her voice sounded pleasant. He was surprised she didn't ask who he was.

Maksym reached for his phone. "Maksym Popov. How may I be of service?"

"Hi Maksym, it's Lenny Osram. We spoke last night at *Im Goldenen Kessel.*"

"Of course. Nice to hear from you." His German was easy to understand.

"Might you and Matviyko be interested in chatting with my brother, Lutz, and me some evening during the week? We'd be happy to see you at the *Kessel* or any place you'd rather meet."

"How about Tuesday, the 15th? Would that work for you?" Maksym asked.

"Let's make it six o'clock. If you want to, bring your wife along. Ask Matviyko if his significant other is interested in meeting us."

"I'd rather not ask. Maybe some other time. Let's do just us four. We'll see you Tuesday." He pressed the red button. Maksym wasn't sure where this new-found connection would lead.

Lenny looked dumbfounded. Maksym was gone. *C'est la vie!*

He texted his brother. "Meet us this Tuesday at six o'clock at the *Kessel.* Maksym and Matviyko are interested in speaking with us. Don't bother bringing Deborah. They want it to be just the four of us."

Lutz had difficulty dealing with his brother's business-like approach in certain situations. For Lenny things were always simple and easy. It was well-known that he could talk without interruption when it came to selling cars; he tended to be short-fused with friends and family. Lutz was a philosopher. Watching his brother manipulate the keyboard on his iPhone distracted Lutz. *How can he do that? I can't even think that fast. Never mind moving those old thumbs.*

⋇

Hans served Lenny his *Altbier* and brought a large bottle of club soda for Lutz. They'd arrived a few minutes before six. Maksym and Matviyko showed up shortly after that. Lenny asked Hans to bring two more beers. He skipped ordering any shots. If they wanted them, the decision was theirs. He had no intention of getting them drunk. Since it was a pleasant night, he had walked instead of calling for a cab. It was only a ten-minute walk. Having all been served, Lenny raised his glass in a toast. "To new friendships."

Maksym raised an eyebrow.

Matviyko looked back and forth—his vision always coming

back to Lenny. Maksym's reaction to meeting Lenny a few nights earlier ran through his mind. Now that he'd been greatly interested in the strangers, he could see what Maksym meant. He chose not to comment on his observations and enjoyed the beer.

After a good half hour of everyone taking their turn at small talk, Lenny signaled the waiter for another round of drinks and some munchies—nuts and pretzels.

At last Matviyko spoke. "My brother shared a bit about our background. Tell us your story. We'd love to hear it." He figured they knew a lot about us; we knew little about them. *Why the interest in pursuing us?*

Lutz responded. "We were born shortly after Hitler came into power. Our mother was Christian, and our father was Jewish. I believe my brother mentioned that Dad was taken from us by the Nazi's in 1943. We never knew what had happened to him. We presume they killed him along with so many others. We had a sister who was born in 1932. Our mother had a hard time dealing with the loss of her husband. After the war, having lost everything, we wound up living with our maternal grandmother in Düsseldorf." Lutz just took a swallow of his *Sprudelwasser* [club soda]. His throat felt suddenly dry.

Matviyko sipped from his beer. "Interesting, very interesting. Tell us more."

"Lenny had a love affair with fancy cars and did well following his dream. I studied jurisprudence and enjoyed my work. I retired from the law firm twenty-three years ago. In later years, I became interested in politics and wound up at the *Reichstag* in Berlin."

"You mean to tell us you enjoyed being a politician?" Maksym set down his glass with gusto.

"Actually, I did. It was an eye-opening experience. But it's all in the past now. My wife, Deborah, and I love to travel. We've both been blessed with good health. Unfortunately, we never had any children. It was a matter we chose not to explore too seriously—a choice we came to regret. That's about it. Nothing really out of the ordinary. Certainly not as exciting as growing up in Yalta and fleeing to Germany."

"I'm not sure about exciting. We've never quite understood why and how we were raised by strangers in a land so far from home. We assume it was a considerable distance because we both seem to recall the long plane ride. Neither my brother nor I have a clear vision of who our family was so many years ago. We remember having a big dog and the Giant Shadow who took us away. While Aunt Sofia couldn't have loved us more than a biological mother, Maksym and I often wondered how different our lives might have been as we grew older. In recent years, we've toyed with the idea of consulting an Ancestry Service only to reject the foolish idea for fear of what we might discover."

"Actually, that might not be foolish at all. On the contrary, it may open doors you didn't know existed," Lenny said. He looked at Lutz quizzically. "You have anything to say?"

"No, not at the moment." Lutz merely nodded, his eyes intently studying Maksym and Matviyko. As hard as his eyes focused on Matviyko's left cheek, he could not detect the birthmark in question. *If these were indeed Doretta's missing twins, Maksym must be hiding the mark under the gray bush of the beard he is sporting.* He had to agree with his brother. There was something about those dark eyes and their noses that had captured his interest. In fact, there was no longer any doubt in his mind that there was some genetic link between the four men.

Lutz looked at the clock in back of the bar. He realized it was past eight o'clock and time for him to give Deborah a quick call to let her know he was on his way. He excused himself before he touched the number on his phone.

Lenny and the others rose from their chairs and headed for the exit. After they made their goodbyes that evening, shaking hands, Maksym took Lutz aside. "If you're interested, you might want to look at a work in progress. For a few years now, I've been trying to piece together notes made by Aunt Sofia which she started recording the day we arrived in Yalta. I smuggled these pages out of the country, never wanting to part with them. Mind you, much of what she said is subject to my interpretation as I'm creating this memoir fifty some years later."

"Why did you have to conceal the writings? Were you searched at the border?"

"Yes. Anything that looked like documentation, they would have taken. Luckily, one of my old-fashioned trunks had a cleverly hidden double floor. But, unfortunately, too many people fled the country for them to search and find."

"How lucky for you," Lutz said.

"I myself kept a journal of sorts and tried to record certain events that impacted our early lives in a strange land. When I finally get to my writing between teaching and doing research, I look for nuggets of interest, leafing through Aunt Sofia's notes and my own. That certainly helps when I try to retrace our lives. My thoughts, putting them on paper as I'm writing today, may not exactly reflect what we thought or how Aunt Sofia or I felt at the time, but I'm doing the best that I can to recreate that time in our lives. It may never be a bestseller, but it should make for fascinating reading."

Lutz didn't need to contemplate. "You have me interested. I'll be delighted to look over what you've written so far. Please jot down my mailing address." Maksym noted it on his phone.

Matviyko kept looking over his shoulder, wondering what kept Maksym. Knowing how concerned Matviyko was regarding their privacy, Maksym would share with his brother the content of his conversation with Lutz at a less threatening moment in time.

Chapter 7

STILL in his pajamas, Lutz retrieved the morning mail lying on the floor by the front door. He noticed a sizable yellow envelope among the pile of letters he carried back to his desk. *It's a good thing that slot is as big as it is.* The package was addressed to Dr. Lutz Osram. He tried to decipher the return address and finally arrived at Maksym Popov, PhD.

I'll be darned. He meant what he said. Lutz grabbed his letter opener and slit the yellow envelope. He stared at the title "The Long Journey"—A Memoir—by Maksym B. Popov. Lutz was impressed by the neatly word-processed manuscript in progress. He flipped open the enclosed note. "For Lutz. Not a stranger, just a friend I hadn't met before. Don't know why but I feel connected to you." It was signed by Maksym Boryslav Popov.

Lutz turned to the next page and read the dedication. "To Aunt Sofia, the woman who became my mom and welcomed us, not as visiting guests but as children, traveling and lost in the world." Overwhelmed with profound sadness, Lutz reached for a tissue and blotted his eyes.

As the lives of the brothers Popov, Maksym and Matviyko,

unfolded before Lutz's eyes, it was the voice of Aunt Sofia that spoke to him first.

⅄

Today is January 23, 1972. As usual, Popov had come home stone drunk after spending the night with his comrades at "The Dungeon," a dive near the Livadia Palace. He is still lying asleep in his bed. Popov must have soiled himself again because I can't stand the stench in his room.

Both men and women have called me pretty. Some said, memorably pretty. I suppose my language skills and looks landed me the job I found. If it wasn't for my work, I don't know how and where we'd live. I still love my position as an interpreter for the many foreign visitors. I speak French, Italian, English, German, and some Spanish, all languages I studied in school. I also learned Ukrainian and Russian at home. My parents died young. I was an orphan at seventeen.

Our front door is wide open and I am staring at a giant of a man, a dark figure, who has invaded our home. The frightening stranger standing before me tightly clutches two little boys by their arms. I have never been close to such a forbidding character. He's a brute. The manner in which he speaks is rough and ugly, like the utterances coming from my husband. I've learned to accept such language from Popov to whom I was betrothed against my will. My father engineered the match shortly before he was shot to death. He had known Popov since the days they both fought during World War II when the Nazis were retreating from Kyiv. I believe it was in 1943.

I became aware Popov could never give me children after we were married. Not because he was twelve years older than I, but because he'd been castrated by German doctors on his eighteenth birthday. They thought he was a dirty Russian Jew.

I learned from the dark man that Popov had promised him lots of money were he successful in finding a child for me to raise. Instead, he pushes the nameless and frightened boys toward me and demands his price. Once I hand him a paper bag filled with countless large bills I found lying on the floor next to Popov's bed, the invader deserts our home. I immediately assumed Popov must have robbed a bank. Where else would he have gotten that kind of money?

The boys look at me with tears in their eyes. They're scared. When I address them in Ukrainian they don't understand a word I speak. I try English and French. Still, there is no response. At last, I speak in my sketchy Spanish and see the smiles on their faces. I tell them my name and ask them for theirs. I realize immediately that Eli and Ed wouldn't do it in Yalta. I had to come up with other names. I am thrilled to have them in my home and want the boys to feel that they are welcome and loved. Not in my wildest imagination had I dreamed I would finally become a mother at age thirty-five.

I touch their faces and then bend down to hug them. At first, they back away from me, a stranger, but they realize I want nothing but to love them. I can read the fear in their eyes. "You must be hungry," I say in Spanish. My Russian-Spanish dictionary helps immensely.

They nod in the affirmative. I make apple pancakes, and they devour them. I was right; they hadn't been fed for days. The boys have as hard a time expressing themselves as I do. Gestures help a lot. "We had soup. It was blue. Maybe it was red. Once on the big plane, they fed us awful bread," Eli finally speaks. "Ed got sick on the plane. He spit out the soup. The bad man beat him." He looks up at me and says: "I like you."

"I'll give you a bath in our wooden tub and wash your clothes.

We need to buy some new things for you on my next day off. But we must be quiet; we don't want to wake Popov, my husband. He's often in an ugly mood. Do you know what I'm trying to tell you?" I ask. Both boys look at me with big eyes.

They don't mind my stripping them naked. The warmth of the water feels good. There are big smiles on their faces. I wash their clothes by hand and am thankful for the windy day. Everything dries quickly on the line in our little backyard. I use one large towel to dry both boys. They giggle as I rub them firmly. Finally, I wrap them in a large woolen blanket, keeping them warm until their clothes are ready to be worn again.

⋈

Popov emerged from the bedroom and looked the boys over. The light from a single bare bulb reflected off his bald head. He used one of his nicotine-stained fingers and picked his nose. He coughed and spit on the floor. I knew he hated speaking in his uncharacteristic high-pitched voice. At times he would expound on the mutilation of his body, cussing anyone in earshot. "Looks like my friend was true to his word. I wonder where he got them. A few months ago, I told him over a beer or two that I wanted you to have a kid. I was tired of listening to your moaning, knowing nothing would come of my screwing you. What are the kids' names? Did he tell you anything when he dumped them off?"

"He didn't say. All he wanted was the dough you promised him. By the way, where on earth did you get that kind of money? Certainly not by working."

"I stuck a gun in the ribs of one of those goddamn rich American tourists who flashed his big money clip while he took a piss at the palace. He didn't know what hit him. I socked him so hard in the gut he passed out. I dumped him in one of the stalls where he probably came to and discovered he'd shit in his pants and had been lightened a bit in the treasure he carried on his body."

"You didn't?"

"Damn right, I did. I'd seen him talking to another guy in the hallway, bragging about how much money he always carried. He said he didn't believe in using credit cards. I decided he would pay the price I owed that bastard for fetching the kid. I never expected him to come up with two. Hope you're happy now that you got these two brats to take care of." He dropped his suspenders and headed for the WC.

I was glad the boys understood nothing of what was said. When he emerged from the bathroom, reeking after his generous act of defecation and the foul smell permeating the little parlor, he returned to discussing the boys. "What do you plan to do with them? Got any idea what ya want to name them? Did he not give you any idea where they came from?"

"None. I told you what happened. Sometimes you don't listen. All he wanted was the money. Where did you meet this character? He gave me the willies."

"Sometimes I'm confused. Who gives a fuck? He got the job done."

I covered my ears. Popov kept glaring at me. "It might have been one of the Mafia who introduced us at the dump where I get plowed every day. And then again, I might have encountered the gangster at the palace. I don't give a shit."

I stood with my mouth wide open. "Perhaps I spoke to him about our dilemma in one of my drunken stupors. The guy took pity on me and the lack of balls. Guess he was serious when he assured me he'd bring back some little bastard from one of his trips to South America."

"You mean he didn't work through legal channels and an adoption agency? You must be joking? I wondered about all the money you gave him."

"Of course, I'm not joking. And no, he didn't work through some *goddamn agency. He stole those kids at a convenient spot and got them out of the country as fast as possible. Human trafficking works that way. He has, on occasion, tried to fix me up with some cute young chick from abroad. I told him not to bother. Adoption agency? You live a pipe dream," Popov yelled at me.*

I walked away from him and hugged the boys. After I dressed them in their washed clothes, we sat and looked at each other. "Aunt Sofia has come up with names for you boys," I said. I looked at Eli "You will become Maksym and your brother will be called Matviyko. Later in school, the other kids probably will rename you, Max, and Matt," I said.

I was almost sure they had to be twins. They were identical in size and coloring and looked very close in age. I thought they might be between three and four years old. Of course, the boys were not old enough to share such information. I was determined to learn as much about the kids as possible. I showed them a greeting card featuring a birthday cake. "When is your birthday?" I asked. There was no response. Still pointing at the card, I tried the universal birthday song.

Eli looked up. "We sing when Santa comes," he said in Spanish.

I smiled. "Close enough. I've just decided on your birth date. It will be January 6th; you two are my Epiphany."

Ж

Lutz put down the pages he had read. *Interesting beginning.* He couldn't wait to get back to his reading of Maksym's memoir.

Chapter 8

Lutz flipped through the pages doing his speed reading. Curiosity took hold of him. Eli and Ed hadn't quite rung true. He was glad Aunt Sofia had established a birth date for the foundlings.

Reading aloud, Lutz struggled to imagine Aunt Sofia during those early days in the boys' lives.

It's now two years later. We had fun celebrating Maksym and Matviyko's fifth birthday. I'm glad they started kindergarten as soon as possible. Their Ukrainian language skills have grown by leaps and bounds. The boys sound as native as the kids in the neighborhood.

I was fortunate to find reliable daycare close to Livadia Palace. Latvia, the young woman, working with Max and Matt after school, is wonderful with them and has taken a special liking to the boys. I'm always greeted by sharing of a joyful event that happened during the day.

"Both boys are doing remarkably well," Latvia told me. "While I'm not discouraging them from using Spanish, their Ukrainian language skills are improving daily. They will have no trouble when they join first grade next year. Maksym does a tad better with making friends

than Matviyko, but I'm not concerned about it. There have to be some personality quirks, even among identical twins.

"I've never met your husband. When I asked Maksym about his dad, he told me he couldn't remember him and that Mr. Popov was not his father. Did I understand him correctly?"

"You did," I answered. "We adopted the boys a little over two years ago. All that is known to us is that their parents were killed in a plane crash, as were their older siblings. Neither Maksym nor Matviyko want to talk about it, which we understand. I've learned not to push them. Let them volunteer what they recall. Then, when they are ready to share information, make a note of it."

"That's good to know. They are just so well-behaved and eager to learn. It's a real pleasure working with both of them."

Those kinds of comments always lifted my spirits. Having Maksym and Matviyko in my life made it easier to tolerate Popov's tirades when he found his way home after the long hours of getting too acquainted with his friend in the bottle. I often wished he would recognize what joy his act of obtaining the money brought into my daily existence. Of course, I never dreamed he would rob one of the visitors to Livadia Palace. After telling him about my feelings when he was drunk or first thing in the morning when he was sober enough to go to work, I eventually gave up on wanting to share my thoughts. I knew he hated himself for having brought the boys into our lives. The idea might have crossed his mind to take some of his frustrations out on them. But, had he ever done so, I would've killed him. Popov never knew I had a gun in my night table and would have known how to use the weapon.

Lutz was stunned by these revelations. He now realized how much the boys meant to Aunt Sofia. Continuing on, he began to turn the pages quickly, reading like a speed demon.

It is now April 2ⁿᵈ, 1979. Maksym and Matviyko were star pupils in fourth grade. Being past age ten, they couldn't wait to start at Gimnaziya Im. A. P. Chekova, one of the renowned high schools in Yalta. I had no worries about their attending a good school. Both boys were bright and received full financial support. I didn't even need to worry about transporting them; it was all handled by the State. I wished Popov would be more supportive, but things went from bad to worse. One afternoon, the police contacted me to let me know they arrested him for disorderly conduct. Apparently, he undressed in the middle of Franklin Roosevelt Street and defecated. Traffic came to a complete stop in all directions.

Lutz almost wet his pants. He couldn't believe what he read. *What a life! What a story!* He turned the page.

I asked a neighbor to take me to the station since I didn't know how to drive. Furthermore, Popov never would have allowed me to use the old jalopy he owned. I had to sign my life away to get him out of jail. The cop who released him informed me that if there were ever another episode of the kind they observed, they would lock him up for sure. How I wished they did.

He didn't spout off while riding in the car with Anton, our neighbor, but I suffered through another barrage of expletives after we closed the front door. He tried to lay blame for his behavior on the boys. Supposedly, Max and Matt, as he preferred to call them, were to blame for the solace he sought by going for a drink. He was a drunkard long before Maksym and Matviyko were in the picture. It was a falsehood to lay the blame at the boys' feet. And, of course, it never was about one drink. I knew him as one of the worst alcoholics I'd ever encountered. My father liked a shot of vodka now and then, but I never saw him drunk.

⋈

Reading on, Lutz made an enlightening discovery. The writing and style suddenly were different from that of Aunt Sofia's. Now, he realized, it was Maksym who wrote the next chapters and providing a different perspective into events in the Popov's home from his own point of view.

At first astounded, then Lutz began to enjoy reading Maksym's account of his early days at the high school in Yalta.

⋈

I began putting words to paper when my English teacher, Mr. Igor Shevchenko, encouraged me to do so. My mentor impressed me. His gray hair and mustache were always trimmed. He never appeared in class without wearing a suit and tie. His shoes were always polished. He was the complete opposite of what we saw in Popov.

The second day at the Gimnaziya was my baptism by fire. Mr. Shevchenko asked us to step into his office. It was I who stared into his questioning eyes.

"You sound different than other boys in class. Why do I have this feeling that you're acting strange and not telling me the truth?" He tapped his desk with a wooden ruler." What are you hiding from me and your classmates?"

My face became flushed. I scratched my armpits, feeling the dampness. I felt nauseous and reached for a handkerchief. I knew what the next question would be.

"It's not your dark hair and eyes that give you away. It's the color of your skin and a certain lilt in your speech that makes you stand out. You're not Ukranian. I hear it in your speech."

There it was. I had to confess. "To be honest, we don't know where we're from. Matviyko and I remember being on a plane for a very long time, and we were flying over a lot of water. Perhaps we came from South America? I don't know the answer. We were only three years old when we found ourselves living with the Popovs. It was Aunt Sofia who insisted to make us part of their family."

He looked at Matviyko. "Is he telling the truth? That's a weird explanation." Shevchenko kept raising his shoulders.

Matviyko was even more flustered than was I. "It's not that we don't want to tell you where we're from; we simply don't know. Neither do Popov nor Aunt Sofia. All we seem to recall is that some strange character dumped us into their lives. When Aunt Sofia insisted on making us part of their family, not too many questions were asked by authorities and few were ever answered in greater detail."

Mr. Shevchenko shook his head. "It's not my place to interrogate you." He turned back toward me. "Maksym, I'm pleased with your writing skills and your ways of expressing yourself in Ukrainian and English. Who cares if you speak with a strange accent?"

Matviyko and I were glad to have the confrontation with our teacher behind us. The next hurdle was a parent-teacher con-

ference Mr. Shevchenko arranged with Aunt Sofia. We made up our minds to be as quiet as a silent movie, or was it acting more like church mice?

The year before we started school at Gimnaziya Im. A. P. Chekova, Aunt Sofia was promoted to a supervisory position of the interpreters program at the Livadia Palace; this gave her a much-needed boost in her source of finances and greater confidence in her own abilities. Although Popov's earnings weren't negligible, much of it was wasted on his nasty habit.

Aunt Sofia had no problem meeting with teacher Shevchenko. Helping her with getting seated on one of the creaky old chairs facing his desk, he began talking about us.

"I suppose, Maksym and Matviyko shared with you the talk we had a few weeks ago?"

"I have no idea what you're talking about. Were they misbehaving or getting into fights with other boys?"

"No. It wasn't anything like that. I was curious about their accent. They gave me as good an explanation as they were able to provide. Apparently, you know no more about their place of birth than they."

"That is correct. What does their accent have to do with their academic performance you wish to discuss with me?"

Shevchenko realized he had touched a nerve. "You are absolutely correct. Maksym and Matviyko perform in all subjects in the upper percentiles. I have no complaints about their academic performance. Perhaps my curiosity got in my way."

Aunt Sofia went on the offensive. "I like my position at Livadia Palace and believe I have the necessary skills to help the boys with their homework. Unlike my husband, I have most evenings free to work with these young men."

"Since you mentioned it, where is your husband in the evenings? Does he have a night job?"

"I hate to say it; he's a drunkard and prefers 'The Dungeon' to our home. I'll make sure that Maksym and Matviyko receive desirable support from me in the home environment. My one and only concern is that the boys obtain as good an education as possible."

"I'm pleased to learn that." Mr. Shevchenko rose from his chair, indicating that he considered the conference concluded.

Aunt Sofia shook hands with the teacher and walked out of his office with us. "Now, that wasn't so bad," was all she said before she rushed out of the building, wanting to catch the bus to Livadia Palace.

Needing to use the restroom we excused ourselves. As we entered the head, Matviyko nudged me with an elbow. "Pretty gutsy how she stood up for us, don't you agree?"

"If she doesn't, I will," Shevchenko said as he stood at the latrine to the left of Maksym. We hadn't heard him following us into the WC on his softly padded shoes. As he zipped up, he made one final comment. "You're lucky to have her in your corner."

We didn't know what to say as we were washing our hands.

Chapter 9

Lᴜᴛᴢ couldn't distance himself from the manuscript. Fascinated, he dove into Maksym's recollections of his brother and his experiences during their earlier years living in Yalta. As Lutz skimmed through the writ in progress, several entries caught his eye.

> *It's Epiphany, Aunt Sofia tells me. Matviyko and I are much more excited about our birthday. It's our ninth. No school yet. Popov doesn't care. No party for those brats, he told Aunt Sofia. She didn't pay him any mind and baked us Honey Babka. It was good, but so sweet our teeth hurt. She sang us Happy Birthday in Ukrainian. We sang along, and sang so loud we didn't hear Popov snore. Aunt Sofia promised to bake Varenyky with cherries for our next party. We laughed aloud when she told us we could help make the treat. Varenyky are boiled in water. We thought they were baked in the oven like any old cake.*

Then Lutz glanced at entries for the next year, 1978. Aunt Sofia talked about May first celebrations. They had never heard of the event before. She made Sochniki for the occasion.

We helped Aunt Sofia with stuffing cherries into the Sochniki pouches. She discovered that I liked sweets. Our faces were covered with cherry juice by the time we were done. She didn't mind the mess we made and laughed with us.

Since there was no school, she shooed us out of the house. Aunt Sofia wanted us to enjoy the parades. I was curious. Matviyko couldn't have cared less. He wanted to catch a soccer match. I asked Aunt Sofia the reason for the parades; she told me it was to celebrate the importance of working people in Socialist and Communist countries. We stood with the others for a while watching the heavy boots of the marchers going past. I thought the music was okay but Matviyko was bored and pretty soon we walked away.

There was an open market surrounded by gardens. A group of men raised the Maypole. I swear it was fifteen meters tall. The pole itself was natural in color with all of its bark stripped off. Borysko, the boss man of the crew, introduced himself to us kids. His biceps bulged under the sleeves of his sweat-stained undershirt. We could tell he was strong. Matviyko called him burly. His full head of red hair and bushy beard got my attention. I could only see his lips, well hidden under the abundance of facial hair, when he smiled. He was pleased to see happy boys and girls willing to help decorate the pole.

He turned to me. "What's your name, kid?" He touched me on the shoulder.

"It's Maksym. The other kids call me Max."

"Max will do. You aren't scared to climb up that pole on those pegs, are you?"

"Nah. It's easier than climbing cherry trees."

"I'll toss you some ropes. They need to be hung from those pegs near the top. Are you sure you want to do this? Does your father know where you're spending the day?"

"No problem, Borysko. He doesn't care. He's probably lying drunk on the floor of "The Dungeon.""

"That's tough, Max. Here's another rope." Borysko reached for a handkerchief in the back of his pants and wiped his eyes. He told me his father was also a mean drunk, who used to beat him, his siblings, and their mother when he came home tripping over things as he walked around in a stupor.

I gestured toward Matviyko. "That's my brother; he wants to help, too. Let those girls do the bottom of the pole." I blushed when I mentioned the girls. Some of them were much sturdier in build than were we.

"Good suggestion," Borysko said.

When the job was done to Borysko's satisfaction, all of us, even the men, danced the Hopak around the Maypole until we fell tired onto the soft grass surrounded by a field of flowers. One of the girls bent down to smell them. She picked some of the blossoms, wanting me to inhale their fragrance. I liked the smell of the irises in bloom. May first turned into a fun day after all. The best part was the Sochniki. I can still taste the cherry juice dripping down on my face.

⋀

Lutz nursed his third cup of cappuccino. He looked forward to learning what happened to the boys as they entered into the next phase of their lives. His eyes caught the word *Gymnasium* (high school) again and awoke in him memories of attending lectures in literature, music appreciation, elements of art, philosophy, and logic.

Having turned ten earlier in the year meant that we would be transferring to another school in late spring. Neither Matviyko nor I knew what changes were in store for us. The best part of being at the Chekhov Gymnasium was that we made some new friends. For whatever reason, we rarely sat next to each other in high school. It didn't matter that our teachers were aware of the fact we were twins. It might have been done on purpose although none of the teachers ever let us know their rationale for keeping us apart.

At first, I shied away from meeting new people, never sure what to say when put on the spot. The question I feared the most was when asked where I was born. It was often the first and most challenging inquiry. Mr. Shevchenko wasn't the only curious teacher.

A boy who sat next to me in several classes was Ivanowich Volodko. His father was a physician. He asked me to call him Ivan when his father wasn't within earshot. At first I didn't understand. Ivan looked different from all the other boys in class. He was taller and his hair was lighter in color. I decided to be nosy. People are always asking me embarrassing questions ran through my head. Why shouldn't I ask?

"How did you get to have blond hair?" I asked and felt at first that I made a mistake.

"That's easy. My grandma came from Sweden. She was my mom's mother. My mom died years ago. She had the feared illness," Ivan said.

I didn't know if I should ask him if he meant cancer.

Ivan Volodko was different in more ways than his looks. He was more interested in discussing a particular play, a piece of music, an author of interest, the pronunciation of an English word, or whatever was of momentary importance to him. I was glad Ivan sat next to me. He was easy to talk to and shared my thirst for learning.

Matviyko had other interests. He met Fedir Bondar on the soccer team. His father came from a long line of barrel makers and was heavily vested in vodka production. Pablo Bioko and Stepan Savchenko were two other boys we befriended during rest periods. Most of us had similar interests and abilities because none would have been admitted to the Gymnasium if we hadn't passed rigorous standard exams.

Then during my third year at the Gymnasium, Ivan invited my brother and me to meet his family. It was an event that shaped Matviyko's and my future.

We discussed the invitation with Aunt Sofia, and she assured us we were safe to ride the trolleybus to Alexander Nevsky Cathedral. The Volodko villa was located near the well-known Catholic edifice. Ivan and his father met us. They were accompanied by Boris, their frisky collie, who was only too eager to make the acquaintance of Ivan's school chums. First he sniffed our shoes. I wasn't sure what he smelled. When Boris licked my hand, I knew I made a new friend. Boris wagged his tail when I ran my hand over the back of his head. Matviyko and I felt at ease with the informality with which we were accepted by Ivan's father.

"Welcome, welcome, young men."

"Dad, this is my buddy, Max," Ivan said. "And without a doubt, this is his twin brother, Matt. They are Maksym and Matviyko but all of us in class stick with the shorter version. It's like no one in our family calls me Ivanowich."

"That may be true, but someday, when you boys are no longer boys but grownup and professional men, you will want to use your full given names because someone gave much thought in bestowing those names on you." Dr. Volodko smiled; he hoped he'd gotten his message across to us.

Lutz stopped reading for a moment. *Guess Dr. Volodko never failed to seize a teaching moment.* He turned the page and kept reading.

Ivan's father looked straight at Matviyko and me. "My wife and I have been looking forward to meeting you." He shook hands with both of us. "There's never a dinner conversation without Ivan telling us of your adventures at school." Just then he bent down and ran his hand across Boris's back. "He loves to get out and walk." Boris was good for another gentle touch by his master. "It's just a short jaunt to our home."

A few minutes later we were facing the house.

"Some people call it a villa, but it's just a comfortable home in my family since my grandfather built it close to the turn of the century. I believe it was actually built in 1905 or 1906. It's not important. It's been home for as long as I can remember," Dr. Volodko continued. He let the dog off-leash. Boris sat down by the wrought iron gate and gave a couple of woofs. "Here we are. That's his formal way of welcoming you." Ivan's father smiled at the dog and us.

An exotic female emerged from the front door. She was much younger than Ivan's father. Her hair was dark and straight and very long. It glistened in the sunlight. A diamond-studded barrette kept the left side from obscuring her face. The right side of the eye-catching crown was tucked behind her ear. Her face was youthful and bore a mere touch of rouge. Her lips were outlined by deep-red lipstick. Her dark and mysterious eyes were those of a Russian Tatar. She smiled broadly. I thought she looked like a gypsy. There were some living in town; Aunt Sofia made a point of telling us who they were.

Ivan's mother extended her hands in greeting us. "Welcome! Now, who is Maksym? I can hardly tell you apart."

"I'm guilty as charged!" I shook her hand. I loved the silky feel. "This is my brother Matviyko. Some call him Matt," I said.

"Come in. Marita is waiting to serve us dinner. She's my trusted housekeeper—hard to find these days with so many women working in shops, factories, or the tourist industry." Mrs. Volodko walked ahead of us toward the dining room. Balancing gracefully on her stiletto heels, her movements caught my eye. Ivan's father held the chair for her. I never saw that done by Popov.

"Ivan tells us your mother heads the interpreter program at the Livadia Palace. Must be interesting work?" Mrs. Volodko asked.

"It is for sure. Sofia is my adopted aunt; we lost our parents many years ago. Aunt Sofia, that's what she asked us to call her, is a wonderful teacher when it comes to languages." I hoped for no further inquiries that might concern our family.

The large round table was set for six. I kept staring at the dishes. I had never seen any like it. Ivan's father told us the dishes were of the blue onion variety often featured in European porcelain makers' collections. Sterling silver flatware, large linen napkins, and crystal glasses rounded out the attractive and welcoming dinner table. I was intimidated by the opulence on display. We had never experienced anything like it in Popov's home. As hard as Aunt Sofia tried, there never was enough money to allow for frivolity.

Matt and I wondered who the sixth dinner guest might be. We didn't have to speculate for long. Varida, Ivan's eight-year-old sister, joined us promptly. She merely curtsied in greeting us and didn't utter a word. She was a miniature version of her mother—

in looks only. Varida looked us up and down with a smirk on her face. I was certain, she didn't care that Matviyko or I were there.

"Ivan's mother died of cancer ten years ago. So I was fortunate that Ayzilya fell in love with me when we met a year later at a conference in Moscow," Dr. Volodko said. He winked at Ivan. "She stole our hearts, didn't she, Ivan?"

Ivan blushed but concurred with his father's assessment. He nodded. It had taken time for him to accept the exotic woman in their midst who now assumed the role of wife and mother. Watching Ivan's reaction to his father's question, I assumed that Ayzilya was decidedly different from his mother.

Ivan's father bowed his head and said grace. "I was raised in the Catholic faith. We attend church at the Alexander Nevsky Cathedral. Do you go to church?" he asked after they finished the prayer.

Matviyko looked at me, a questioning frown on his face. "We never go to church, and no one ever graces a meal. Popov, who married Aunt Sofia, says he's an atheist. His God lives in a bottle." Matviyko knew he should not have shared that.

"Are you trying to tell us that the man who adopted you is an alcoholic? That's terrible. Did you call him Popov?" Ivan's father asked.

"Yeah. That's all he's been to us in the ten years we've lived with them. We never knew him by any other name. He's mean to Aunt Sofia. She adores us."

"Do you recall anything about your mother and father? What about siblings? Did you have any?" Ayzilya asked.

I knew those questions would be asked sooner or later and was tempted to decline an answer after Matviyko kicked me not so subtly in the shins. But quickly, I changed my mind. "Matt and I remember a long plane ride and a giant of a man who accompanied us. From what we've been told, our entire family, parents and a brother and sister, were killed in a plane crash in early 1972. All I can recall is this enormous shadow of a man who left us with the Popovs. It was Aunt Sofia who insisted on adopting us," I responded.

My body language spoke volumes. My face had turned beet red. I considered the subject closed. I did not want to share that I had come to suspect that we had been abducted from another country. When I fell victim to my nightmares, it often seemed like I viewed certain events in our past lives through a murky fog. I didn't want anyone to know about the many nights I cried through the years when I wondered who my real family was. Seeing the happiness in Ivan's family made me realize how much I missed in life. Now and then as I sobbed into my pillow, I would hear Matviyko sniffle in the background.

Dr. Volodko turned to me; I sat on his right. "Ivan tells me you're interested in writing. Are you familiar with Anton Chekhov? He spent much time in Yalta, where he wrote some of his best-known plays. We might want to visit his former home. Today it's known as the White Dacha."

"I would like that. I believe our school was named in his honor."

"That's correct," Ivan's father responded. "You will enjoy visiting the museum dedicated to the great Russian playwright. You know, of course, that he was a physician first. He's often quoted, having said 'Medicine is my lawful wife, and literature is my mistress.' It's a shame he died so young; he only lived to be forty-four. Chekhov loved living in Yalta, enjoying our beautiful landscape and the beaches by the Black Sea."

"Why do they call the sea black?" I asked Dr. Volodko. "The water isn't black."

"*The question is often asked. It has nothing to do with the color of the water. Historically, many pirates and criminals controlled the land surrounding the large body of water. It was seen as unsafe. Not today. So don't hesitate to enjoy the beauty of our beaches.*"

"*We won't. Matviyko and I like to swim.*"

Matviyko was glad when he could change the topic of conversation. "Fedir, Stepan, Pablo, and I are into soccer. What can you tell me about the soccer teams in Yalta," he asked.

"*I'm not aware of any soccer clubs in Yalta at this time; of course, most high schools have their teams and Fussball has become quite popular. Glad to know you're involved in physical activities. I always have to push Ivan to become interested in some sport.*"

"*Guess he's a bookworm like my brother." Matviyko nudged me hard with his elbow.*

Ayzilya saw what was happening. "Boys, no bad behavior at the dinner table. If you want to pick on one another, the three of you cool off in the backyard. I know all about boys. I had six brothers." She stopped talking. Tears were smudging her eye makeup.

Ivan's father spoke. "Four of them were much older than my wife and they were all killed in our last war. The other two, who are still alive, are both serving in the Navy."

The party ended with an invitation to join the Volodkos for Mass at the cathedral and Sunday dinner soon. Dr. Volodko laid a hand on my shoulder as we were saying goodbye. "We can see that you boys don't have it easy at home. Your aunt sounds like a lovely lady. Popov is another story. We want you to feel welcome at our place any time."

Ivan, his father, and Boris walked with us to the trolley. We shook hands and gave Boris a goodbye pat on his back before we hopped on the tram. Having shown our pass to the conductor, we sat down. Matviyko spoke at last. "What did you think? A bit different than at Popov's, eh?" For once, I had to agree with him.

Chapter 10

Deborah and Lutz sat at the breakfast table, having another cup of coffee while leafing through the *Rheinische Post.* Lutz stared at the headline. "I don't know what's coming from this situation in Ukraine." He covered his eyes with both hands. Visions of Auschwitz-Birkenau flashed through his mind. He never knew where his father had been taken in 1943. "My God, if mother had not hidden us away, we might have been among those who were slaughtered. I know all about anti-Semitism in Russia. It may not end with Ukraine. Putin is mad enough to threaten world peace. It's no longer saber wrestling; we are talking atomic and biochemical warfare. He scares the hell out of me. When that madman killed himself in 1945, leaving our country in ashes, we swore there would never be another war like it." He placed his hands on Deborah's.

She grasped them firmly. "I'm sorry to see us face the possibility of World War III. Let's be fervent in our prayers when we enter temple this weekend. I've prayed every night since this horror started. That's all we can do for now." She decided to change the topic.

"How are you coming with the reading of Maksym's manuscript? Both he and his brother must be worried about friends and loved ones they left behind. Are you still thoroughly engrossed in his writings?" She took a sip of her coffee and the newspaper in her lap dropped to the floor. She couldn't help seeing the headline. "Are you closer to discovering who those men are?" Deborah said softly.

"Not unless we find a way to see the birthmark on either Maksym or Matviyko that Doretta spoke about in her 1968 letter. Or, I suppose, we could delve into this ancestry thing called 'MyHeritage DNA.' Otherwise it's going to be difficult to make any such determination. So I just have to be patient and keep going, and Lenny has to dig further into those family slides. No question about it. Those boys had very interesting experiences while growing up in Yalta. Even though their home environment was a mix of the good and the bad, the discovery and ultimate connection to the Volodkos put their lives on a more positive track."

"It all sounds pretty intriguing. If Maksym ever brings that memoir to fruition, I'll suggest it to my book club."

"On that note, I'd better get into the shower before I've frittered away the most productive hours of my day." Lutz got up, tightened the belt of his robe, and kissed Deborah.

"Well, dear, I guess I am looking forward to learning the latest in the lives of your foundlings," she said.

As he headed off in the direction of their bathroom, Lutz hummed, *"Morgenstund hat Gold im Mund"* [The morning hour bears gold in its mouth].

Lutz sat down at his uncluttered desk and opened the manuscript. Maksym's opening sentence caught his attention.

Trouble in paradise. The occasion to reconnect with Ivan's family arose quicker than I could have imagined. It was early in the morning of September 19, 1981, that Aunt Sofia's phone woke her from a deep sleep. Loud as it was, the shrill ringing got our attention. We jumped out of bed and charged for the extension in the kitchen. The connection was bad. Matviyko held the phone so that I might hear what was said. We could hardly make out what the husky-sounding male was asking.

His name sounded like Officer Lupinsky, and he kept asking if she was Sofia Popov. Once she confirmed in her sleepy voice that she was indeed Mrs. Popov, there was a lengthy pause. We detected her heavy breathing as she listened intently to what the officer told her. She covered the phone and ordered us back to bed. Matviyko hung up the extension in the kitchen. We kept looking at her, a questioning expression on her face. It was obvious that Aunt Sofia was shocked by what the man was saying. We couldn't take our eyes off her as we lay watching from our mattress just thrown on the bare floor. Finally, she rubbed the "sand" out of her eyes with her left hand and reached for her glasses. Aunt Sofia looked for a pad and a pen. She was writing down some information. When she hung up the phone, she spoke to us.

"It's bad. Popov was involved in a head-on collision with a city trolleybus. He was pronounced dead at the site of the accident. While the trolley was badly damaged, no one, other than Popov, was killed or seriously hurt. The ambulance driver who took him to the morgue stated that Popov was intoxicated. He wrote in his report that he was drunk as a lord."

Sofia frowned, the last utterance of the speaker finally sank in. She was speechless. Aunt Sofia didn't cry; other recipients of such sad news might have. Aunt Sofia coughed to clear her throat. She told us that she had to leave for the morgue as quickly as possible to identify the body before they could release it to the Krematoriy.

Sofia dressed without making any further comments. To an outsider, she would have appeared cold and detached. She was anything but. Aunt Sofia slipped into a light-weight raincoat and then spoke. "I'll take the trolley to the police station and the morgue and can walk to the Krematoriy. They are only a couple blocks apart. Closer to the hour of opening, I will call my supervisor at Livadia."

Matviyko and I decided to get up. The night appeared to be over.

"Make sure you eat something before you leave for school." She gave us a quick peck on the cheek and was out the door.

I feigned waking up by rubbing my eyes. Matviyko was wide awake. "Can you believe that he's gone? I thought I wasn't hearing right when she gave us the news. An accident! In the morgue? Next they finally get rid of him in the Krematoriy." I couldn't believe my brother. He seemed totally detached and as cool as a dish of ice cream on a hot summer's night. He had no difficulty rattling off the facts to me.

I stared into space, not fully grasping the implication of what happened. I couldn't bring myself to say out loud what I felt at hearing of Popov's unexpected death. So instead, I whispered a quick prayer and thanked God that it wasn't Aunt Sofia who was struck down. I wondered if I should make the sign of the cross as I had seen Dr. Volodko do.

Then reality took over. There was a more important matter. I was starving. "What are we having for breakfast?" I asked. My stomach was growling. Rarely did we have to fend for ourselves. Unfortunately, this was one of those days.

Matviyko searched the icebox and found some leftover waffles. He opened the covered dish and showed me his found treasure. "They'll do just fine after we stick them into a frying pan," he said. He was always handier in the kitchen and often watched Aunt Sofia when she was cooking. I couldn't care less. I'd much rather read an intriguing book than getting involved in cooking.

When Matviyko placed the reheated waffles in front of me, I covered them heavily with plum jam. I loved the deep purple color. I knew it would be tasty. I'd seen Aunt Sofia make it from scratch.

"Don't eat so fast. Have some of the milk I poured for you. Will you ever learn to chew your food?" Matviyko admonished me.

I couldn't wait to get to school and share the news with Ivan. "You'll never believe what happened. Popov died during the night. He had a collision with a trolley. We don't know all the details. The police hauled his body off to the morgue. He must have been driving that old jalopy of his. Aunt Sofia told us what the cop said. I'll know more tomorrow," I whispered. I didn't want the other boys to hear what I had to say. I must have been nervous. My shirt was soaked with perspiration.

My hand was all over my face. "Stop picking your nose," Ivan said to get my attention: "That's bad. Maybe there's something we can do? Knowing my father, he would want to help. Sounds like Aunt Sofia will have her hands full. You mind if I tell my dad?"

"Why not? Tell him, for sure!" I burst out. "Aunt Sofia will take all the help and support she can get. I know I should feel sad, but I don't. Popov was such a miserable and nasty man. I firmly

believe the three of us will be better off without him." I wondered what Ivan thought of my speaking so freely.

"From what I know about the man, I agree. However, I won't quote you to my father. He's forgiving, sometimes too forgiving for my taste—too Christian. I'm not always willing to turn the other cheek as he asks me to do," Ivan said.

"Exactly my feeling," was all I had to say.

Aunt Sofia's phone rang that evening just as she came home from work. She was fearful of lifting the receiver, never knowing what was next. She slipped out of her coat and handed it to me. She nodded in the direction of the closet. I made sure it was put on a hanger. She reached for the phone.

He spoke before she had a chance to say a greeting. "It's Andriy Volodko. Sorry to learn of your husband's death. Ivan came home with the sad news after school. You have our sincere sympathy. How may we be of help?"

"That's kind of you, Dr. Volodko. I dislike saying it, but my departed husband wasn't a nice man. He didn't deserve to die the way he did, but he would never listen to the voice of reason. May he finally rest in peace."

"Let him rest in peace, indeed." Andriy made the sign of the cross. "Do you need help with the final arrangements? Are there any legal matters in which we could assist you?"

"There won't be a funeral or a memorial service. Popov was a self-proclaimed atheist. Because of these circumstances, and the fact that he was badly mutilated, the coroner recommended immediate cremation. Thus the quick action at the Krematoriy earlier this day. I'm not sure yet what to do with his remains.

The boys and I may go for a steamer ride on a less stormy day and release his ashes into the Black Sea. Right now, I can't think of what to do." She took deep breaths before she continued. "I'm thankful to God for having Maksym and Matviyko in my life. They have truly been a gift from Him."

"Are there any financial issues facing you?" he asked.

"I believe Popov's insurance will cover the damage to the trolley. Thank goodness, no one else was hurt. But thank you for offering to help."

"When you and the boys are ready, let us know. My wife and I would like to meet you. After that, we'll plan on having dinner at our house. Go well," Andriy said.

"Thank you, Dr. Volodko. The boys still talk about their wonderful time with you and your family. Maksym was enchanted by your beautiful wife."

He smiled into the phone. "I have to agree. Ayzilya is indeed beautiful," Andriy said.

"I look forward to meeting you and your loved ones. Have a pleasant evening." Aunt Sofia replaced the receiver with care. The frown gave way to an expression of relief; a hint of a smile fled across her face. Ivan's mother is fortunate, she thought.

Chapter 11

DEBORAH was in a culinary mood and opted to fix Lutz a special lunch. She had ordered his favorite lox from *Die Kurve* the day before and knew how well he liked her homemade bagels. Through the years, she had become quite the chef in Jewish cuisine. Neatly arranged on an onion-pattern blue and white Meissen plate, lox, bagel, a dish of cream cheese, sliced onion and tomato, with parsley and capers as garnish were pleasing to her eyes. She hadn't taken her apron off when she surprised him sitting bent over Maksym's manuscript in his elegant office.

"Surprise! I thought you could stand a break. You've been working much too hard. But, of course, I know better than that. It's really not working. You're having much too good a time delving into the mystery." She winked at him.

"Oh! That looks delightful. You succeeded in surprising me. How about joining me with a glass of Prosecco?"

"Would love to, but I'm going to be late for a meeting with the gals. We want to check out some options for the Seder. You enjoy. I'll see you later. Just do me a favor and rinse your plate before putting it in the dishwasher. Now, give me a kiss and be a good boy."

"Isn't that a left-handed compliment to make to an eighty-eight-year-old codger." He kissed her softly on the lips. "I'm about to try reaching Maksym by FaceTime. Wish me luck."

She heard only part of what he said as she walked away.

Lutz consulted his contact list and touched the app on his phone. The response was instant.

"Well, isn't that a surprise?" Maksym smiled. "The marvels of technology. Who would have thought of this possibility ten years ago?"

"Steve Jobs did wonders for us. On the other hand, there are days when I detest the invasion of my privacy at all hours of the day and night. For me, it's a love-hate relationship. I'm really into your manuscript. I just learned of Popov's untimely death. Sounds like he was a real piece of work," Lutz said.

"As you've guessed, he wasn't loved by anyone but barkeepers and sleazebags. Looking back on those early years, to be honest with you, Aunt Sofia, Matviyko, and I were better off without him in our lives. He lived a miserable existence and tried his best to infect us with his misery."

"That's the way I see it. Glad to read about the connection you made with Ivan's family. Are you still in touch with him?"

"Yes, we are, very much so. Ivan studied medicine at renowned medical schools in Ukraine and did further studies and residencies in Tübingen, Germany. He specialized in obstetrics and gynecology. Even before we finished our *Abiturs*, Ivan talked about nothing but wanting to bring new life into the world. His father always encouraged him. It was the specialty Andriy would have chosen had it not been against his father's wishes."

"How so?"

"His father was into bones; he thought delivering babies belonged in the domain of midwives."

"Hmm. Strange notion. I presume Ivan is married?"

"He met his wife, Ulyana, in medical school. She's a surgical nurse and works with him in his practice. He lost his dad a few years ago. Mrs. Volodko, Ayzilya, is still alive and lives with them. Ivan's sister, Varida, fled Yalta shortly after we did in 2014. She lives in Frankfurt, and we see her now and then on holidays or special occasions."

"I'm happy you still have that connection. Lenny and I were wondering what you thought about meeting Aunt Sofia at Kaiserswerth? Would she or you have any objections?"

"Off the top, I don't believe she'd have an issue with us coming to see her. I mentioned meeting you at *Im Goldenen Kessel* when I spoke with her by phone the other day. She's still very much with it; it's only her hearing that challenges her on occasion. I'll clear it with Matviyko. He's the quirky psychiatrist in the family. He always looks at the glass as half empty; you know what I mean, don't you?"

"I actually do; Lenny can be that way. *Must run in the family* crossed Lutz's mind.

"I'll text Matviyko and will get back to you—*pronto.*" *Now where did that come from? I haven't spoken Spanish in ages,* Maksym thought.

Matviyko's response was prompt and surprising. "If you're okay with it, so am I. I'm scheduled to chair the orals of one of my doctoral candidates. Please, make all the arrangements." He touched the red button, grabbed files off his desk, and charged out of his office.

Lenny had offered to drive his Mercedes since they were to meet the brothers Popov in front of the *Kessel.* Matviyko had advised Maksym not to divulge their locations to people they knew so little about. Maksym agreed to abide by his brother's conditions although he didn't share his conservative attitudes. Matviyko had no idea that

Maksym had mailed a copy of his memoir in progress to Lutz Osram since they last met at *Im Goldenen Kessel.*

There was little small talk during the ride to Kaiserswerth. Someone spoke of the low water levels as they crossed the Rhein and the dry winter they'd enjoyed. There had been frigid days and some snow, but nothing like what they'd experienced in other years.

Maksym closed his eyes and envisioned the splendor of the golden rapeseed fields he recalled when he'd driven out to Kaiserswerth the previous May. The brightness of those blindingly yellow fields was still deeply embedded in his memory.

They entered the residence for senior living and headed straight for room 1258 on the main floor. A distinct odor of antiseptics and cleaning solutions hung in the air. However, Maksym was certain the residence was kept clean and safe.

Aunt Sofia received her boys with open arms and kissed them on both cheeks. Then she stood back and eyed the elderly gentlemen in their company. None of them caught the introspective smile that crossed her face quickly. She took a deep breath because she could see the resemblance between the strangers and her boys as if someone had shown her photos revealing the images of the four that were captured at identical ages. She was tempted to pursue the subject out of curiosity but opted not to during this first encounter. *No, no, don't share your discovery with the visitors. They each will have to have their own Epiphany,* Sofia thought.

She extended a graceful hand with the inevitable signs of aging. Liver spots and prominent veins were in plain sight. Her smile was infectious and sincere. The hair bleached almost white by long years of living was fashioned into an elegant French twist. She wore large amber earrings, the clip-on variety, inherited from her grandmother in Ukraine. She bought the sleek necklace fashioned in silver and amber at Livadia Palace while she worked there. Her dress was simple but classic and tailored from a mauve bouclé. She stood ramrod straight; Aunt Sofia was the epitome of class and elegance. Maksym looked upon her with a particular pride.

Sofia was hesitant to speak. "How nice to meet you. Maksym called me and told me about becoming acquainted with you." There was that mysterious smile again. "It's good when people see something in each other at first, even as strangers, only to discover that they are destined to become friends who simply hadn't had the chance to meet along life's paths." She winked at Lutz and then at Lenny.

"Well said," Lutz commented.

Both Lenny and Lutz read between the lines. Then, finally, they realized Aunt Sofia had made the connection. Lutz was tempted to speak further but held his tongue.

Aunt Sofia pointed with her cane in the direction of the glassed-in balcony. "Knowing you were coming, I arranged for coffee, tea, and some pastries to be brought to my table on the terrace. I love sitting out here on sunny days. The staff here is highly accommodating."

"I'm pleased to hear that," Maksym said.

Matviyko merely nodded.

"These days I'm happy you convinced me to move here. I couldn't handle living by myself any longer. It's good you live so near. And when you are too busy at the university, I know I can count on Daryna to take care of whatever I might need."

She looked at Matviyko. "I often pray that you'll find a soulmate yet, Matviyko." She couldn't understand why a handsome man in his early fifties wouldn't want to be married and have children. Yet, Sofia often wondered why she hadn't searched for another man after Popov's death.

Matviyko connected with her eyes. "Marriage was never on the top of my list of desires. Deep down in my soul, Popov killed those feelings and needs. I have strong relationships with members of both sexes, but I would never want to be bound to another to that degree. Let's leave it at that."

"That saddens me to hear. Be so kind, and hand me the jacket lying on the ottoman. I feel a tad chilled."

Matviyko obliged and helped her get into the sleeves.

She reached for the dainty handkerchief tucked into the left pocket of her quilted wrap. A seamstress who had also fled from Yalta years ago had tailored it for her.

Matviyko couldn't let it go. "Stop wasting your time praying for me, Aunt Sofia." His face reflected worry. "Pray for all we left behind when we fled to the West eight years ago. Putin is about to make his final move on our country. He suffers from delusions of grandeur. Satan, Napoleon Bonaparte, and Hitler wander through his soul and occupy his mind. As a result, the man is driven by insanity."

All were taken aback by Matviyko's last statement. "You know how to put a damper on things, don't you, my brother?" Maksym asked.

"No. Not a damper. Just a realistic view of things the way they are about to unfold. You're the eternal optimist; I'm the opposite. Professionally, I've encountered too many characters with the same issues plaguing Vladimir Putin. I read him like a book to use that cliché."

Maksym assisted the old aunt with getting seated in her favorite chair on the balcony. The spot allowed her to stay in visual touch with her visitors while beholding a forest of ancient trees in the background. She loved the airiness of her glassed-in four-season veranda.

Sofia realized where the conversation might drift. "Come on, gentlemen. Let's not let the coffee and tea become cold and no longer enjoyable." She reached for the coffee urn. "Who prefers coffee and who would care for tea?" She had removed the coffee pot from the silk-brocade coffee cozy and admired the china pattern. "It's lovely," she said and smiled.

"Coffee for us," Lenny and Lutz spoke at the same time.

"Same for us, as you well know," Maksym said.

"Guess I'm the only tea drinker these days. Don't be shy, gentlemen. I don't want any leftovers. The pastry chef does a wonderful job. These strawberry tarts are delicious. The berries must come from some greenhouses in warmer countries."

"Perhaps South America, New Zealand, or Israel," Lutz speculated.

She selected two pieces for each of her visitors, placed them on pretty gold-rimmed china plates, and then spoke before she took her first sip of Earl Gray. "I would like to learn something about you two gentlemen. Help me. You are Lutz, and your name is Lenny, right? You must forgive my shortcomings. I've grown old and my ears don't always listen well." Sofia beamed at her visitors.

"You remembered correctly. You are doing just fine. But, let's not forget, the three of us have the best parts of our lives behind us," Lenny responded. "I'm the bachelor in our family. Lutz and I were born in Essen but have lived most of our adult lives in Düsseldorf except when Lutz studied to become an attorney. I just made it through my *Abitur* and went into business, a very successful and lucrative business.

"Our father was Jewish and our mother was Protestant. He was taken from us by the Nazis in 1943. We believe he perished in one of the concentration camps. We were nine years old. That tells you something of our age."

"Oh, that's terrible," Aunt Sofia said. She saw the tears in Lutz's eyes.

"Mother and her three children barely survived the war. We were lucky that she succeeded in hiding us in the darkness of the underground bomb shelter for weeks on end. Who knows? We might not be around to tell the tale. After World War II, we lived with our maternal grandmother near this city for a long stretch. Our sister, unfortunately, died in 1973."

"That's so very sad," she commented again, shaking her head in disbelief.

"My significant other, Anna, passed away not too long ago. These days I live alone in a much too large place for someone my age. But, not willing to move into a facility like this, I'll probably die there. Now and then I'm envious of Lutz. He has Deborah who brightens his days. But, unfortunately, I never pursued the kind of talents he has. He's like our sister; she loved to read and write. And, of course, he never truly retired. Sometimes I wonder if he should have rerun for office." Lenny felt he'd revealed too much.

Aunt Sofia was curious about the sister Lenny mentioned but decided it was best not to ask too many questions. She could wait if Lenny or Lutz were willing to go into greater detail. An inner voice told her there was more to this serendipitous discovery between these four men than any of them realized. She was hoping for more but had learned to practice patience. The wheels of justice turned slowly, but the truth would always reveal itself in the end. *What do the Germans say?* She pondered. *"Die Sonne bringt es an den Tag,"* [The sun shall reveal it in the light of day]. She nodded. *There's some truth to that.*

Chapter 12

Maksym awoke just before sunrise. He was once again bathed in perspiration. "Damn it, not that nightmare again," he mumbled. None of it made any sense. At one point as the face of the Giant Shadow hovered over him, he thought he could touch it. No matter how hard he tried, he couldn't penetrate the darkness of the glasses that sheltered the creature's eyes. He always thought it had to be a man.

He jumped out of bed. Daryna would know he'd suffered another troubling night. Maksym hoped a long session in their sauna would clear his head. It didn't. He dressed in a running suit, hurried to his office, and grabbed his cell. *I need to speak with Matviyko. My God, he was there with me. Why doesn't he remember any of this? Never mind that he does not remember; why isn't he plagued by the horror of it all the way I've suffered for years? What if I'm making all of this up in my mind? Am I going crazy?*

Matviyko picked up his phone, detecting the vibration. "Whenever you call at an ungodly hour, I know it means SOS. What's up, my dear brother? Are you in trouble?" He raised an eyebrow.

"Am I in trouble? You got that right. I'm in deep *kakka*. I had that damn nightmare again. It was different in some ways." Still feeling the heat from the sauna, he yanked off the top of his running suit and reached for a clean t-shirt. Not wanting to lose his connection, he slipped it over his head with his free hand.

"How so?"

"I was surrounded by Spanish-speaking people. Then we had those interactions with our father on the phone. I liked his voice. I saw our mother—not clearly. I think it was she. Wasn't Mom tall and slender?"

"You're asking me? For some reason I don't recall all these details. Remember, it's you who is having all these confusing memories in your world of mixed up dreams."

"I swear, I could smell that Chanel perfume Daryna likes so much. I never can remember what number it is."

"Write it down. It's Chanel N°5. What's so difficult about that?" His brow was furrowed.

"It's like I have a mental block about certain things. The slender woman in my dream sang that prayer from the opera the reviewer in the paper raved about not too long ago; you know that children's thing with the kids getting lost in the woods. It was all so real."

"You mean "*Hänsel and Gretel?*""

"Yeah. Exactly. It bugs me that I cannot keep that title in my head. Am I losing it? What's wrong with me?" He wiped the sweat off his forehead with the back of his hand.

"No, you're not losing it but you suffer deeply every time you relive those scenes in your subconscious state of mind. You keep searching and searching instead of letting your mind forget about it. You're not going into that dark night again, are you?" Matviyko closed his eyes, wondering how he might help his brother.

"The worst was the encounter with the Giant Shadow and being put into that black sack. God, I could feel that slimy thing all over my body." He shook his body, wanting to free himself of the disgusting experience. "I strained to see the bastard's eyes but couldn't penetrate the darkness of his sunglasses. I screamed out loud and awoke the moment our plane headed for the inevitable crash."

"Of course, you know that crash never happened or we wouldn't be here to talk about it. In your nightmares, what supposedly happened to our family so long ago, becomes what happened to us. We'll never know." Matviyko kept rotating the phone on his right cheek; he was becoming more annoyed by the minute.

"There's got to be a means of cutting through that veil of uncertainty. I didn't tell you. I've gone to see a psychic, wondering if she could put me in touch with our loved ones through a medium. I know, you'll say it's all a hoax. But I've become desperate."

"Gosh, you're going from bad to worse. Where and when did you do that?"

"Right here in town. Not long before we met Lenny. I couldn't help seeing the sign advertising her services. She's on the north side of Graf Adolf Platz."

"You better go for a swim and clear your head. Have you discussed any of this with Daryna?"

"No. And I don't want to. Sometimes she thinks I'm going crazy. Other times she wonders if I'm fabricating the whole *megillah* [story]. It's best kept between us." He inhaled deeply. "I better share this with you; I sent a copy of my manuscript in progress to Lutz. He told me it makes fascinating reading."

"There you go again. Why did you see the need to do that? Nothing will come of it." Matviyko shook his head. He was pissed. "I really don't grasp what you see in these men. Yes, there's the question of a noticeable resemblance to us, but that doesn't mean that we are related. Let's face it, we've all encountered our double or two in unexpected places. You're just making too much of this. I can see why Daryna is worried about you."

"You really can't see it? There's something about Lutz and his brother that draws me to them. I can't explain it. You, of all people, the great psychiatrist, should know and understand."

"My attitude has nothing to do with my profession. These exchanges and meetings with Lutz and Lenny have reawakened the matters so deeply buried in your subconscious mind. I feel for you and am glad I'm not plagued at night the way you have been so often. If you want to consult with a shrink, I'll refer you. You know it's unethical to treat family." Matviyko considered the case closed. He was ready to touch the red button.

"Thanks for your professional advice. I don't need counseling; what I seek are answers to the many questions that lately haunt me almost every night."

"Perhaps one of my colleagues should try hypnosis. The circumstances have changed since we were in our early twenties. You're much more mature." Matviyko knew he was trying his brother's patience. "Dr. Walter Ungeheuer, in my department, is internationally known as a specialist in hypnosis. I'd be pleased to arrange it for you. Just say the word."

"What did you say this guy's name is? Ungeheuer? You must be joking."

"What's wrong with his name?"

"Why would I want to be hypnotized by someone called *Monster*? If I had a handle like that, I'd change it in a heartbeat. And a professional? No way!" Maksym was tempted to call an end to this conversation.

"So what's in a name? It's his business. Maybe he thinks it fits his profession. It's weird that I never put two and two together," Matviyko admitted.

"My God; this reminds me of Herr Professor Doktor Unrat." A smile crossed Maksym's face.

"Who the hell is that? I've never heard of him."

"It's because you never studied German literature. Heinrich Mann wrote a novel about a *Professor Unrat,* who was anything but disorderly as the name implies. He was the epitome of propriety. His downfall was that he fell in love with a harlot. Marlene Dietrich played the part of Lola Lola in the 1930 movie *Der Blaue Engel* [The Blue Angel]. It put both Mann and Dietrich on the international map and gave them world-wide recognition and notoriety."

"So what are you trying to teach me now?"

"My intent is nothing like it. It's just that you're so damn narrowly focused. All you can think of is your work and developing the next important project to find new tests for exploring the human mind. I've never seen you read a book for the pure enjoyment of reading."

"Are you suggesting I'm ignorant?"

"No. Not that. Sometimes I wonder why you went for psychiatry. One of my professors told me years ago that most people who enter into the field are half nuts themselves and are looking for answers to their problems. Maybe that was your way of dealing with the issues I'm facing."

"What makes you think *I have* problems with some people in certain situations?"

Maksym was glad they weren't speaking in person. He felt totally disgusted. "It's because you still haven't mastered German the way I have. That's OK. You do just fine in your job. No criticism intended." He knew he wasn't speaking the truth. "All I want to say is, I don't need your goddamn hypnotist, and for sure not one named *Ungeheuer.* I don't know how to explain it, but I feel it in my bones; there is a connection between us and Lenny and Lutz Osram. I saw the expression on Auntie's face when we walked into her place. She could sense the link that binds us. Let's just give it more time."

"It's not time you need. You need help. Sorry, I can't give it to you."

"I'm not asking for your help. I just want you to understand what I'm trying to learn. Trust me! Trust my instincts."

"Okay! Okay! I get it! You keep talking to Lutz to your heart's content. Who knows, he might have the answers to your questions. In the meantime, I'm freezing my ass off." It was only then that he realized he'd gotten out of bed without his pajama bottoms. "If you're done with your early-morning pontificating, I'm crawling back into bed. By the way, Julia spent the night with me. She's keeping the *Federbett* warm." He touched the red button not wanting to give Maksym another chance to react.

Chapter 13

Lutz studied Maksym's papers, digging his way through numerous triumphs and tragedies on the soccer field involving primarily Matviyko and his buddies Fedir, Pablo, and Stepan. An episode describing the young men's introduction to the creation of vodka at Fedir's father's distillery after the boys turned sixteen caused Lutz to laugh aloud. The affair brought back an event long forgotten. He could still see Lenny and himself being totally sloshed the last year at the *Gymnasium*. One of their teachers had invited a bunch of young men to a party at his house. They had gotten the *Schnapps* and cigar treatment with similar results. His eyes turned back to Maksym's papers for a second look.

Today is June 13, 1984. What happened yesterday must be remembered. I suffered for close to ten years living with my caretaker, Popov, a miserable drunk. It was enlightening to learn how one of his favorite libations was produced. Why did one of our friends have to be associated with alcohol production? Fedir arranged for a tour of his father's plant. When we arrived, huge trucks were delivering grains needed to produce the desired elixir.

"It could've been half-rotten potatoes at some other plant. You think the grain smells are bad? Those fermenting spuds would knock you for a loop. You'd never drink ordinary vodka again," Fedir challenged.

I let him know we never had tasted the stuff. Within seconds I regretted saying what I said. Mr. Bondar, Fedir's father, had overheard my comment.

He scratched his bearded chin. "You haven't lived until you've tasted my very special kind of vodka. You boys come to the tasting bar and I'll initiate you in the finer art of drinking."

A fatal mistake. We were served three different flavors of vodka and were shown how to down each enormous shot glass in one swoop. To us they were sizable vessels for certain. After the third round, Mr. Bondar presented us with cigars. "All good vodka drinkers enjoy an excellent cigar. I'll make strong men out of you boys yet," his voice booming and echoing off the walls of the cave stacked to the ceiling with casks of vodka.

Fedir's father was a huge man and probably could have imbibed all night without becoming stewed. Neither my brother nor I had ever put away a single glass of hard liquor, and certainly not three of that size in short succession. The cigars were the final coup. We baptized the tasting bar sufficiently with vomit. Mr. Bondar cussed but had no one to blame but himself. Enlisting our help in cleaning up the mess we created was a wasted effort. He had to do it all by himself. Aunt Sofia made us strip and put all we were wearing, including our tennis shoes, into her washing machine. She let us know that she didn't need reminders of past events. We understood what she was telling us in not so subtle terms. In our boyhood, Matviyko and I never touched vodka and cigars again, especially after seeing Popov returning home stone drunk every night.

ᛊ

Lutz put down the manuscript. He went to the kitchen and fixed himself a hot toddy. He was fully aware of the power of suggestion. He also knew he would not be drunk after one drink. *I wonder how Maksym would feel about a different approach?* Tapping his desk while waiting for Professor Popov to pick up his phone, he formulated what he wanted to say.

"Maksym Popov speaking; how may I be of service?"

"Hi Maksym. It's Lutz Osram. I'm really into your writings and have an idea. I have nothing but time on my hands and always felt I was related to Sherlock Holmes. How would you feel about meeting with me on a regular basis and talking about the events that shaped your lives? It will be more powerful to hear you tell it or have you highlight some of the details in person."

Maksym hesitated for a second. "Matviyko thinks I'm gullible to be so open with you. He's always been fearful of strangers. Perhaps that early-childhood trauma haunts him more than he's willing to admit." He took a couple sips from his coffee cup. "Matviyko always acts like macho man when I open up about my nightmares. The thought occurred to me on occasion that he went into psychiatry to discover himself. But to come back to your question, I would very much like to have your input on the manuscript."

"What do you think of my suggestion?"

"Wednesday afternoons I'm completely free. We could meet at my office, or perhaps I should see you at your home? It might be easier on you not having to maneuver traffic, finding parking, etc."

"Deborah would feel easier if you were to come here. My office is pleasant enough, and we could talk as much or as little as we felt like. How about next Wednesday? Want to make it two in the afternoon?"

"Two o'clock it is. You can count on me. I'm excited about today's lecture since I'll be discussing Wagner's fascination with Medieval characters and the link of King Ludwig II of Bavaria to Wagner's operas. But you probably don't care. Got to run. My next lecture is in ten minutes. *Adiós.*"

Lutz wondered why he didn't sign off with *Aufwiedersehen.* He regretted not having a chance to respond.

☙

Deborah responded to the doorbell. She gasped as she looked Maksym in the face, believing she was looking at Lutz when they first met forty some years earlier.

"Anything wrong? Are you not feeling well?" Maksym reached for her, believing Deborah was about to faint. She was as pale as a ghost.

"Oh no! I'm perfectly okay. Must be my age. On occasion, all the blood seems to drain from my head, making me a bit dizzy."

Maksym studied her. Deborah's hair was as white as fresh-fallen snow and was pinched in the back by a carved amber clasp—simple but stylish. Practical, too. She wasn't made up and showed just a touch of lipstick. Her eyes were a translucent aquamarine. *Lovely, even in her eighties,* he thought.

She smiled. "Lutz is expecting you. I'm so glad you met. Not practicing law any longer, he's got too much idle time on his hands. I wish he would write again. It used to give him so much pleasure. He was a regular sleuth. Agatha Christie was his idol." She walked ahead of him toward Lutz's office. It was the click clack of her heels on the parquet floor that alerted Lutz that someone was approaching his office.

"Sorry. I didn't even hear the bell. Must have nodded off for my *Mittagsschläfchen* [midday nap]." He was about to rise from his chair when Maksym gestured not to bother. "Please, don't get up." He walked around the desk and shook Lutz's hand. He was surprised by the firm handshake, considering Lutz's age.

"I'll leave you to your work," Deborah winked. *Work? It will be pure pleasure for Lutz.*

Maksym's eyes were drawn to the intricate design of the rosewood desk top, a geometric pattern of inlaid wood of different shades and covered with a heavy glass plate. He couldn't help running his hand across the smooth surface.

"You can touch it. Can't harm it. I always loved that focal point in my office. Grab that large red wingback. The leather has been worn down to a softness that comes with old age. Many an anxious butt has graced it through the years. Just relax. We'll talk."

"What did you mean by anxious butts?"

"Prospective heirs often sat in that chair, waiting with bated breath to learn how much or how little—and sometimes nothing—was left to them by a dearly departed."

"That's quite a story-telling chair," he winked at Lutz.

Lutz acknowledged the comment with a nod, wishing to change the topic. "You mind if I use a recorder? It will be a tad easier on this eighty-eight-year-old noggin." Lutz tapped his head with his index finger.

"By all means. When I studied at the Crimean Humanitarian University in Yalta, I often asked permission of my professors to record their lectures. Rarely was there an objection. It helped me immensely with my studies."

Lutz touched the record button on the machine discreetly seated on his desk. "From what I've gleaned so far, you are both still struggling with your early lives. Do you have any idea where home was before the shadowy figure came on the scene? On occasion you seem to think home was in a Spanish-speaking country?"

"True. Quite a few years ago when Matviyko was working on his doctorate, his mentor tried hypnosis on us. We agreed, hoping we'd make some serious discoveries. We did respond to Spanish stimuli but we could never discover the country from which we originated. All we know is that it was somewhere at a considerable distance because of the long flight we do seem to recall. It's often been suspected that it might have been Chile. But that's all just pure speculation. Nothing concrete."

"Tell me about your friend Ivan Volodko and your connection to that family. You implied earlier in your writings that the Volodkos shaped your life. In what way?"

"Andriy, Ivan's father, as he insisted we call him in later years, was a true renaissance man. He loved life and was always only too willing to share his fortunes, his knowledge, and his many gifts with those whom he loved. Aunt Sofia and my brother and I were blessed to find ourselves among the throng of special people in Andriy's all-too-short wanderings on this earth."

"How so? Share some of those events with me. Obviously, the man had a significant impact on you. I've had people like that in my life. My grandmother influenced many directions I pursued. She was a wise old bird and lived a long and challenging life."

"Andriy was shaken to the core when he discovered what a terrible existence all of us had, living with a man like Popov. When he died, we were just thirteen. He was concerned that Aunt Sofia didn't have the means of allowing us to get a good education. Fortunately, that wasn't the case. She earned a good living at Livadia Palace, and we garnered good grades and didn't have to pay tuition.

"When we needed anything out of the ordinary such as certain books, lab materials, clothing, he'd take care of it. Ayzilya, his wife, always insisted that Aunt Sofia and we partake of all holiday meals with them. While Matviyko didn't share my love for opera and the theater, he didn't miss out on anything that involved his interests in sports activities.

"Not long after Popov's death, Andriy wanted us to become familiar with the famous place where our aunt worked. Aunt Sofia was not permitted to give private or free tours of Livadia Palace. Varida, Ivan's sister, was too young to join Ivan and us when the Volodkos took us on tour. I can still hear Andriy as if it was yesterday."

"'The palace was well-known as the summer retreat of Nicholas II, the last Russian Tsar. The estate had been the summer residence of the imperial Russian family since the 1860s. It was this famous palace in Yalta where the fate of Europe following the eventual end of World War II was decided by Winston Churchill, Franklin Delano Roosevelt, and Joseph Stalin.'"

Lutz looked up. "That was the Yalta Conference held on February 4 to 11, 1945. Strangely enough, two days later the city of Dresden was turned to ashes. It was unnecessary cruelty against the people."

"I remember Andriy talking about more than twenty-five thousand people dying. Some wondered if the decision to destroy Dresden was made at the conference. Andriy's eyes reflected the sadness in his heart. He had visited the crown jewel of Saxony during a visit to Germany before the Nazis came to power."

'Why can't the world ever be at peace? I cannot remember a time when there wasn't a war fought somewhere on this earth. It's all so senseless.' Andriy had tears in his eyes.

"He stood at the head of the large oval conference table and pointed at the chairs where the three men sat while staking their claims on Germany after its ultimate defeat. Roosevelt sat in the middle, Churchill to his right and Stalin to his left. It's often been discussed who or what determined the seating arrangement."

Lutz caught Maksym's eye. "I wonder where and by whom the fate of Ukraine is being decided at this very moment. Nothing seems to change from one generation to the next. Dictators and leaders come and go. No one seems to learn anything from history." Lutz took a sip from his drink. "I don't think I could deal with another war and fathom what might happen to those who follow us. World War III must be avoided at all cost." Scenes of horror flashed through Lutz's mind. The gruesome images of Auschwitz-Birkenau and Berlin lying in total ruin blurred his vision momentarily. He wiped away the tears running down his cheeks. Lutz shook his head feeling the strong need to return to the present.

"Andriy would have been devastated by what happened eight years ago in Yalta and, far worse, by what is about to happen in 2022. He was such a peace-loving individual. Andriy was born to be a medical doctor and lived religiously by the Hippocratic oath. Medicine was in his blood. He was so proud when Ivan couldn't wait to fill his shoes.

"As I said in my introduction, Andriy Volodko was a true renaissance man, he was a man who loved culture and all that the word conveys. Ivan and I would never miss a play by Chekhov or a flight to Odessa with the Volodkos in their private plane to attend an opera.

"Of course, when invited for Sunday dinners or any holiday celebrations, all of us attended services at the Alexander Nevsky Cathedral. In the early days, he'd walk us through the edifice and point out every piece of art and tell us anything he knew of significance pertaining to a given painting or sculpture. Andriy viewed these walks through art history as critical to our general education. He didn't want us to become technicians but well-rounded individuals cast in his mold. I don't know if I ever measured up to his expectations but I surely tried."

"I wish I would have had an opportunity to know the man. Interesting! Interesting, indeed," Lutz interrupted. He was thankful Maksym had agreed to the in-person sessions. Hearing Maksym tell his tales placed them on the stage of reality.

"I remember an outing to Gaspra on the Black Sea. Andriy wanted us to know the history of the "Swallow's Nest," also known as the "Castle of Love," a spectacular structure reminiscent of castles on the Rhein or those built by King Ludwig II of Bavaria. On a clear day, one can see it in the distance from Yalta. We had the closeup and personal introduction with Ivan's father as the tour guide. These are moments with Andriy I will never forget."

"Deborah and I were on a Black Sea cruise and stopped in Yalta. Our tour guide pointed out the "Swallow's Nest." It looked like a magnificent structure, sitting on the very edge of the cliff. Sorry, to break your train of thought," Lutz apologized.

"No, no. Not at all. I'm thankful for the many visits to Kyiv and Odessa. Although a transplant from an unknown and distant land, Andriy and Ayzilya taught me to be proud of my adopted homeland and to appreciate its beauty and cultural landmarks." Maksym was moved by the statement he had just made. He wiped away his tears with a handkerchief retrieved from the back pocket of his slacks. "I'll take you up on that cognac you offered me earlier. Just thinking what Putin might do to all we hold dear in Ukraine frightens me."

"How true. I never forgot what Essen looked like in May of 1945. Ninety-five percent of its inner city was flattened. The synagogue, although heavily damaged by Nazi vandals on *Kristallnacht* in 1938, was one of the few major structures that survived all the bomb attacks. I had my belated bar-mitzvah at that synagogue," Lutz volunteered.

Maksym hadn't realized that Lutz was a practicing Jew. "Are you attending temple regularly?" he asked.

"I have for many years, and we keep *Shabbat* and certain holidays in our faith. I didn't when I was younger but eventually longed to honor my father. I'm grateful that Deborah converted to Judaism. Some might refer to me as a secular Jew although I see myself more as a Reform Jew. We don't keep kosher and women sit with men. Many women play a role within the temple. That was important to me and to Deborah."

Maksym noted the prayer shawl hanging over the back of Lutz's chair. "Is that scarf of any significance?" he pointed at the embroidered cloth.

"Oh, that is my prayer shawl. I always wear it to temple and for certain functions here at home."

"Hope you didn't mind my curiosity. I know so little about Judaism. We were often told in Yalta to stay away from Jewish people." Maksym cleared his throat. "This has been a delightful afternoon. Let's do it again next week," he suggested.

Stiff from sitting at his desk for a few hours, Lutz wished his cane was handy. He hated to admit it, but age had crept up on him. "Let me walk with you to your car. A bit of fresh air will do me good. I enjoyed our afternoon together and look forward to next week." He accompanied Maksym to his parked car and shook hands. "Go well," he said as Maksym hopped into his shocking-yellow VW Beetle. *Those were the days,* he thought and turned around. *You are lucky. Lenny probably would have dragged you off to his former dealership. He would have called that cute bug a worthless piece of shit. It's all in the eye of the beholder.* He strolled back to the house, watching every step he took.

Neither Lutz nor Maksym could have imagined that the invasion of Ukraine by Russian troops would occur within twenty-four hours.

Chapter 14

Lutz turned on the *Tagesschau* [early morning news], not believing what he saw and learning that the Russian invasion of Ukraine had commenced only minutes earlier. The event's impact was brought home by the instant transmission of graphic imagery of war. Shells were striking buildings; civilians fled from their homes; women, children and old men hovered under snow-covered barren trees shielded only by cloudy skies promising more snow. Bone-chilling cries of children filled the air. Lutz shivered feeling the pain of many Ukrainians.

He called Lenny, knowing how little he cared about what happened in the world. Once his brother retired and sold his lucrative business, he only watched sports events. Nevertheless, he enjoyed having an occasional beer with his twin. Lutz often listened to Lenny saying he didn't care if the rest of the world passed him by. In his opinion, he couldn't change a thing; why bother one's mind with things one couldn't control or alter.

Lenny looked at his cell phone and realized it was Lutz calling. He glanced at the date and time. It was Thursday, February 24, 2022, at nine o'clock in the morning. "Hello. Why are you calling me this early? The sun is barely up." He squinted toward the drawn silk shades.

"Well, for once, turn on the damn TV and see what's happening in the world. Genghis Khan Putin invaded Ukraine just minutes ago. It's terrible what his henchmen are doing. I feel for Maksym and Matviyko and their friends. Maksym spent yesterday afternoon with me, and we enjoyed learning more about each other. Mostly I think about him. He's agreed to see me Wednesday afternoons to discuss aspects of his memoir in progress. I've essentially agreed to be his ghostwriter—not that he needs one. I think he likes venting with me."

"I can't believe what you are doing. You're way over your head. Do you ever remember how old you are? My God, man. Wake up!" Lenny had walked to the front door and retrieved the morning paper. He didn't believe the headline: **INVASION OF UKRAINE BY RUSSIAN TROOPS IMMINENT.**

"I'm fully aware of my age when I sit on my duff for too long. In the meantime, I'm thoroughly enjoying working with Maksym. For now, I'm letting him do most of the talking. When the time comes, I'll share with him what we have been suspecting. I hope you're right. There will come a day when we might want to invade your turf and raid the evidence box. If you're too embarrassed to have company, don't be so goddamn cheap and hire a cleaning lady. Lord knows you can afford it."

"Yes, brother dear!" Lenny touched the red button and made the German gesture of calling his brother an asshole. He was glad not to be doing FaceTime.

Lutz was glued to the television in his office. Channel surfing among competing news broadcasts, he could see live coverage of bombs exploding in the Ukrainian capital. The graphic images struck fear in his heart as Russian tanks moved toward Kyiv. Thousands of women, children, and elderly clung to what they could carry as they fled toward neighboring countries, searching for shelter and security. What he saw took him back seventy-seven years. Not in his wildest imagination had he expected to see another war like this appearing on Europe's horizons. Up until now, his own generation had come to believe that their leaders had learned their lessons from the devastation of World Wars I and II and all the wars and invasions that had occurred since.

After he'd encountered Maksym's answering machine, Lutz reached the department's secretary. She informed him that Professor Popov had a nine o'clock lecture in Medieval German Literature. Lutz thanked her for the information and left his telephone number, asking to be called back. He felt the need to connect with his new friend. Wanting to make sure his message got to Maksym, he followed up with a text.

Maksym saw the message while he was still in class. It stated that Lutz wanted to speak with him. So, naturally, he touched the green button as soon as he closed the door to his office. After that, he was free to converse for the next fifty minutes.

"Hi, Lutz. This is Maksym. Thanks for calling. I'm just sick to my stomach right now. As much as I knew it was going to happen, it's still hard to swallow. I had a hard time staying on task during my lecture this morning. Discussing Tristan and Isolde as portrayed in Wagner's opera became irrelevant." Maksym looked at his coffee cup and walked across the hall to the restroom. He dumped the stale cup of brown liquid down the toilet but didn't flush. He didn't want Lutz to think he'd taken a leak while still on the phone. Instead, he poured himself a fresh cup and doused it generously with cream. "This could very well spell the end of my country—my people for that matter. It makes me very sad and angry."

"Know that I'm with you. I'll say extra prayers in the temple. We'll talk real soon. If you feel like seeing me sooner, please don't hesitate. I've got a pretty good idea what's troubling your mind." Lutz touched the red button. He didn't have the heart to say more. Lutz longed to hold and protect him like a lost child in the woods.

⋈

Maksym promptly rang the doorbell at Lutz's house at two pm on March 2. The war had raged for close to a week. Little else was dominating the news. So Lutz was surprised that Maksym showed up at the appointed hour. The thought crossed his mind that Maksym might be too preoccupied with the war in Ukraine to even think about his manuscript of the memoir.

Walking toward his office, Lutz spoke, his words riding across his shoulders. "Have you heard from Ivan and his family? They must be concerned."

"I tried FaceTime earlier, but he didn't answer his phone. He might have been at a hospital doing what he's known for."

"Why not try again? It might give me a chance to meet your lifelong friend."

Maksym touched the FaceTime app. A masked female came into view and addressed him in Ukrainian. "Dr. Volodko asked me to respond. He's just delivered twin girls who presented with complications. He'll be with you momentarily." She carefully balanced the phone with her gloved hand so that Ivan came into view. He shed bloody gloves and a heavily stained gown. Last, he removed his mask and reached to hold the phone himself.

"Sorry, Maksym. I thought it might be you calling. I had to do an emergency C-section, but all is well now. You need to pardon my appearance. I look as if I came off a battlefield. Speaking of battlefields, we're all worried about family in Ukraine. I have uncles, aunts, and cousins in Kharkiv and in Kyiv. We've not been able to get through to them."

"That's what I remembered. What about Ulyana? Didn't she have family in Odessa?"

"Yes, and we are very much worried about them. It's such an important port. Putin certainly has his eye on it next. The whole thing is frightening and has turned our lives topsy-turvy. You must be pleased you left Yalta when you did," Ivan said.

"That's for certain," Maksym answered.

"I know Varida is. We talked last night. My sister is glad she moved to Germany when she did and said she couldn't handle another war with Russia. So what do the Germans think about our latest debacle?" Ivan asked.

"It's always front page news and the first thing the talking heads on TV bring to our attention. Speaking of front-page news in our lives, I want you to meet my new friend, Dr. Lutz Osram. He's a retired professor of German Literature and Writing. He is interested in helping me edit the memoir I'm hoping to finish one of these days."

Maksym caught Lutz smiling as he held the screen up to his face. Then, there was a distinct pause before Ivan uttered his first words in German.

"Hallo, Herr Professor Doktor Osram. It's my pleasure to greet you. My German is a touch rusty from lack of use." It wasn't the rustiness of his German that caused him to pause. The strong resemblance between Maksym and his new friend caught his eye and shocked Ivan into speechlessness. He decided not to comment on his observation.

"That is nice of you to help Maksym with his writings. But he needs a push in the right direction to bring this thing to fruition. He's been talking about publishing the memoir for years. I look forward to what he says about my family and me. We have considered him and his brother part of our clan since they were barely out of short pants. And that's a few years."

Lutz gave Ivan the victory sign and turned the phone back to Maksym.

"I better let you go. Your patients need your attention. We'll talk later when you're home," Maksym said.

Ivan concurred and just waved before ending the conversation. The connection to Yalta was gone.

"That's what I love about 21ˢᵗ Century technology. It's marvelous how we can reach out to people many miles away from us," Lutz said. "And even see them. And it doesn't cost a penny."

Maksym couldn't resist. "Of course, we must be relying on Apple devices."

Lutz grinned at Maksym. "Care for something to drink before we continue with your story?" Lutz took his seat behind his desk and reached for the recorder.

"I'm fine just now. I'll pour myself some club soda if I run dry in the mouth. I don't dare have anything alcoholic. I'm glad you're willing to do this. It's taking my mind off current events. We're all concerned about what will come next. Varida called me last night. She and Daryna talked about families in Kyiv who are threatened. This whole thing is totally unreal and scary."

"Watching the news is eye-opening business. During the waning days of World War II, people only knew what happened by what they observed with their own eyes. There was no such thing as live coverage. People went to the movies and witnessed what the government would share with the public. It was always snow from yesterday—filtered old and gray news. Now it is bloody in technicolor and hits you right where it hurts. War reporting has become so real and instant that some of us are impacted to a much larger degree. I feel like I'm experiencing PTSD by watching the events unfold. Just think how these poor people are suffering." Lutz closed his eyes for a moment.

"Are you sure you want to do this today?" he then asked.

"It will be good. Speaking of happier days will take my brain in a more positive direction. But, by all means, let's continue talking about my memoir," Maksym said.

"My questions can wait. I have nothing but time on my hands. Well, that's not really true. My days are dwindling down to a precious few," Lutz grinned as he pushed the button on the recorder. "Let's talk a bit about your education. We were close to the days when you boys were ready to finish high school."

"We had excellent teachers at Gimnaziya Im. A. P. Chekova. Teachers challenged us to do our best not only in subjects in which we were interested but to have an open mind to broaden our world views. As a result, the three of us graduated with highest honors when we finished our *Abiturs* shortly after our seventeenth birthdays.

"One of us might have mentioned it earlier, but being as close as we were to our respective families, we attended the Crimean Humanitarian University in Yalta for our undergraduate work. Aunt Sofia and the Volodkos were pleased that we chose to remain near them for a while longer. None in the family, except Andryi, had an easy life.

"Eventually, Ivan moved farther away when he pursued medical school at Bukovinian State Medical University (BSMU) in Chernivtsi in western Ukraine. Matviyko and I pursued graduate studies at Taras Shevchenko National University in Kyiv. Matviyko got his MD before completing his residency in psychiatry. I obtained my PhD in modern languages with an emphasis on German and French literature. It was Aunt Sofia who instilled in me the desire to become multilingual. Ivan and I often wrote to one another at great length in German. We practiced on each other every chance we had during visits home while he was interning in Tübingen."

Maksym saw a folded map of Ukraine published by AAA lying on Lutz's desk. "You mind if I open it? I could point at the different places in Ukraine. It might reinforce the size of the country. I believe it's not quite twice as big as Germany."

"I hadn't realized that," Lutz responded.

Maksym unfolded the map and then used a ruler to show Lutz the distance between Yalta and Chernivtsi. "When Ivan was in med school, he was almost twelve-hundred kilometers away from us. In those days there was no FaceTime and calling was prohibitively expensive."

"How well I remember," Lutz nodded. "You mentioned earlier that Matviyko took a position at an institution in Odessa. Did he remain there until you fled Ukraine in 2014?"

"Yes. He liked the place and enjoyed teaching and doing research. Odessa provided him with many opportunities to meet colleagues from all over the world. This was especially true after the cruise industry discovered the city's cultural treasures. He hated leaving the country but refused to stay behind when we wanted to make the move to Düsseldorf."

Maksym pointed at Odessa on the map. "Have you been to Odessa? It's a beautiful city." He pointed at a photo of the opera house shown on the back of the map. "It's not among the largest in the world but it is competitive in beauty. It has wonderful acoustics."

"Deborah and I were in Odessa a few years ago but never made it to the opera house. It was dark at the time."

"That's too bad. You might have been able to tour it." Maksym shook his head.

"How did Matviyko fare with German?"

"He was never as comfortable speaking it as I was. He's still challenged on occasion. Matviyko has little problem with professional lingo, but he's not at ease in a social environment. That was a major roadblock for him in landing a teaching job. So I became his private tutor and purposely didn't take a full-time position until one was offered to him. Luckily, we had some savings; Aunt Sofia wasn't poor, and we received financial assistance from the German government. In the end, we made the right decision. He'd have a hard time making a move now."

"And you taught for several years at Crimean University in Yalta, the place where you started, right?"

"It was the ideal place for me to be. I could look after Aunt Sofia, whom I eventually viewed as Mom. Let's face it, she was the one who raised us and loved us as much as any biological mother could have. Remaining in Yalta also afforded me many opportunities to be with Ivan and his family. I was very much affected by the death of Ivan's father. So I was glad both Daryna and I could be there for Ivan, Ulyana, and Mrs. Volodko, the mysterious Ayzilya." He smiled. "I can't resist. The meaning of her name in Tatar is *clear as the moon*. It's almost poetic."

"Such a beautiful name it is," Lutz commented.

"It fit. She was and is radiant and beautiful."

"When I first read your description of Ayzilya, I couldn't help thinking of and comparing her in looks to Aida Garifullina, the show-stopper at the Vienna State Opera. We saw her recently in Antonín Dvořák's opera."

"You mean. *Rusalka?*"

"Yes, yes! That's the one. She has an amazing voice and is beautiful and exotic in appearance," Lutz responded.

"Now that you mention it, I agree. There is a certain resemblance. Although, of course, Ayzilya never sang but neither can deny their Tartar heritage." Maksym entered Aida Garifullina on his phone.

"Just look at her. She's gorgeous." Lutz pointed at the cover page of an opera magazine lying on his desk. "You need to catch her in the final scene from *Andrea Chénier*. It's on Youtube. She and Bocelli recorded it at the Roman Colosseum. Talk about sublime," Lutz said.

"Guess we're both opera buffs. Of course, it's all Andryi's fault; he instilled that love in me. I still miss him badly. He became the father we never had." Maksym reached for the bandanna in his back pocket.

Lutz got up and stretched his arms and legs.

Maksym focused on his host. He rose from the red leather chair and grasped for Lutz who seemed to have lost his balance for a split second.

"Getting on in years," Lutz said. As they walked toward the foyer, Maksym couldn't help seeing their images caught in the full-length mirror facing them. For the first time, he saw Lutz with different eyes; he realized he was looking at the man he might resemble at a much greater age. *My God, he could be my father.* He shook hands with Lutz and smiled. "I can't wait to see you next week. In between, say a prayer in the temple for the people of Ukraine."

"I will. Go well." Lutz closed the door with a gentle touch. *I caught that look on your face. I believe der Groschen ist endlich gefallen* [I believe the coin dropped at last; I think he's finally seen the light].

Lutz walked back to his office and headed straight for the bar. He poured himself another cognac, brought his nose gently over the tulip-shaped glass, and sniffed. His hand swirled the drink slowly as his mind raced. He looked out the window and remembered the sadness in his sister Doretta's eyes when he last saw her. Blinking awake from his daydream, he smiled at his reminiscence, gave the cognac a second nose, and sought out the comforts of a leather sofa. "Now, that feels just fine on my ancient tush." He looked at the grandfather clock and wondered what kept Deborah. *It must've been another exciting afternoon of discussing the latest bestseller.*

Chapter 15

MAKSYM was glad he hadn't driven his car. He couldn't even recall exactly how long it had been since he had last gone running. His favorite destination was the esplanades along the Rhein River. If it hadn't been for the chill of late winter, he would have stripped down to nothing and taken a cooling dive into refreshing waters. Amazingly, he still remembered the hidden location of the spot where he and Matviyko had gone swimming years ago. They often had felt like little boys and, because it was always late at night, no one could see them as they disappeared beneath the waves of the Rhein.

This time, instead of the desired dip, Maksym sat down on his favorite rock and pretended to be Rodin's *Thinker*. No one watched. No one listened. In the resounding silence he was able to commune with the Almighty. *My God. What was that all about? It hit me like a brick. I couldn't believe what I saw. I felt as if touched on the shoulders by a higher being.* Even now he could still see their reflections in Lutz's mirror embedded deep in his mind. *Too many questions, too few answers.*

He knew they had gotten to a point in their relationship demanding he dig deeper. Rethinking what transpired in a matter of weeks,

Maksym realized that it wasn't he and his brother who had reached out, but Lenny and Lutz were the ones who sought them out that evening at *Im Goldenen Kessel. They must have had a good reason for speaking to total strangers. And yet I never felt they were strangers from the moment our eyes first met. In fact, from the very beginning I was especially drawn to Lutz and didn't hesitate to speak with him. And it was I who had chosen to be an open book unlike my brother who turned inward after fleeing our adopted homeland. I often wondered if Matviyko's insecurities had become worse because of his difficulty in speaking in a foreign tongue.*

Maksym reached into his pant pocket and retrieved his cell. He touched FaceTime and smiled when his brother accepted.

Maksym having his back to the river, Matviyko knew where his brother stood. "I see where you are. You're not planning to take a dive, are you?" Matviyko asked.

"No! It'll be getting dark pretty soon and, besides that, it's too darn chilly. I had another heart-to-heart with Lutz this afternoon. He's very much concerned about the events shaping up in Ukraine. Lutz is into reading and editing my manuscript. He's concerned about those we left behind because they mean so much to us."

Matviyko coughed; then cleared his throat. It was his way of voicing disapproval.

Maksym knew what his brother was conveying to him without saying a word. "He is an excellent source and a good editor. Don't forget his background. I called you because I saw something this afternoon as I was getting ready to leave. I was supporting Lutz as we were walking side-by-side toward the foyer. I couldn't help seeing our images reflected in a large mirror down the hallway. He must have seen me stare at us. I have the identical color and shape of eyes and our noses look as if we were cloned. I swear there is some kind of a link between the Osram brothers and us."

There goes that cough again. I know Matviyko believes I'm way off the mark. Why does he persist in being so damn uncomfortable with my relationship to Lutz?

He opted to confront his brother. "Why are you such a doubting Thomas? I just thought you might want to know. I'll play Watson for a while. I better head home; night is descending. Want to meet at *Im Goldenen Kessel* on Friday? I may know more by then. Varida Face-Times with Ivan or Ayzilya every night. I'll let you know if I have any news." Maksym ended the conversation. He was sure Matviyko was on his second beer and couldn't care less about the latest discoveries.

Maksym's mind drifted back to his earlier discussions with Lutz. *He was right in what he said about the impact of live coverage. War is pushed into our living rooms 24/7. There's no escaping. Some news stations are so brutal that our eyes are forced to witness people as they are decapitated or their bodies torn to bits and dragged away in black or white body bags. I can almost smell the stench of decomposing, rotting remains of humanity.*

On the other hand, newsreels in black and white were much kinder to our psyche. He slid off the rock and started to run. He picked up his pace once he was beyond the esplanades. Pushing himself to the limit helped to clear his mind.

He passed several cafés and pubs. People were eating, drinking, talking, and laughing. Unfortunately, no one was paying heed to the images flashing by on the screens mounted on large walls. No one realized the pain that invaded his heart. He wished he could help those they had left behind in Ukraine.

⚔

Lutz hadn't spoken to his brother in more than a week and was pleased when he answered his phone. "Here's hoping I'm not interrupting some important sports event you're watching? I felt we needed to catch up."

"No, no. I'm nursing a beer and listening to the latest on the radio. I can't handle watching those dreadful images they transmit from Ukraine. It's hitting too close to home—even after seventy-seven years."

Lutz needed to change the direction of the conversation. He didn't want to be reminded of his troubling thoughts by his brother. "Are you making any new discoveries in the treasure trove?"

"I keep reading Doretta's letters to Mom and Grandma and have digitized all the slides Fernando sent after Elijah and Eduardo were born, including the beautiful images he sent from the Antarctica trip. There are many good slides by our nephew, Mario, too. I thought the three of us would enjoy watching them some night. Also, I have a nice bottle of wine that deserves sampling."

"That sounds terrific. I feel as if I'm getting to a juncture with Maksym and his brother that we may want them to know what we suspect. I'm still waiting to get close enough to Maksym to see the birthmark. I wish he didn't have that forest of a beard hiding what I'm looking for. If I don't get a good look at it, I might suggest to both of them that we consider DNA testing and wait for the outcome before we have a showing and revealing at your place. What do you say?"

"Since you've gotten so chummy with Maksym, why don't you grab the bull by the horn and ask him if he's hiding a birthmark under that beard? What harm can it do?"

"I'm not ready to do that. I'm not sure he'd be ready for that sort of a shock without my having more facts to convince him."

"By the way, I didn't gloss over your hint of having the revelations staged at my house. Why my place?" Lenny asked.

"I've got my reasons." Lutz made a gesture as an aside that his brother would not have appreciated. He was suggesting Lenny was dense.

Lenny was still dealing with the DNA idea. "OK, then. DNA testing is a good option. Just make sure you cover all the legal angles involved before you give and share samples of DNA. You know Germans and *Datenschutz* [privacy issues]," Lenny said.

"Don't worry. I'm still up on what's happening in my profession. If Maksym and Matviyko are willing to do it, I'll ask Martin, my neighbor, to be a witness to the procedure. You know he's involved in that DNA business?"

"Yes, I remember," Lenny replied. "You be careful," he warned. "I still don't understand why you insist on me having the eventual show and tell at my place?"

"Yeah. And why not? You have a lot more space than we do. You are the one with the large dining room that's rarely used these days," Lutz said.

"You have no idea what's involved. My place is a dump. I can't recall the last time it was dusted. No way will I let strangers come calling under those circumstances."

"What do you mean dump? It just needs some loving attention from a mop and a dust cloth. Don't be so cheap. You can afford to hire help."

"I suppose I can." Lenny became annoyed by his brother's interrupting phone conversation.

"Well, I'd better let you go back to the news. We'll talk later." A touch on the phone disconnected Lutz. He'd learned to love his handy phone and would never be without it. Times certainly had changed.

Lutz set down the phone and reached for the evening paper. He learned it was easier to digest the latest in the ongoing debacle in print than watching live footage transmitted from Mariupol or some other devastating battlefield.

He picked up the empty snifter and frowned at its emptiness. *I hate to admit, images of war and people fleeing ahead of bombardments take me back to those grizzly days in the bunker in Essen. Sounds and smells of the place haunt me in my dreams when those scenes are reawakened by modern reportage. I experience those moments in living color during many a restless night.*

Lutz sought consolation in a touch of *Rémy Martin. Asbach Uralt* wouldn't do the trick tonight. He poured himself a stiff drink and held the glass up to the light, admiring the warmth of the color. Lutz took a hearty swallow and lifted the crystal snifter to his own reflection in the gilded mirror facing him. "L'Chaim," he smiled before he took another uncompromising sip.

Chapter 16

It was Friday, April 1. Lutz and Deborah ushered in *Shabbat* with the traditional meal. The sun had set when they sat down at the table. He always loved watching her as she moved her hands gracefully well above the candles and directing the warmth and light toward her face with her palms. She spoke the prayer in a hushed voice. *Barukh ata Adonai, Eloheinu Melekh ha-olam…* flowed from her tongue.

Lutz remembered Henrietta Blumenthal. She had taught Deborah well when she went through instructions prior to converting to his faith all those years ago. The two women had met through a book club they joined during the 1970s. Henrietta was years older than Deborah, but it was friendship at first sight.

The older woman had survived her incarceration at Theresienstadt (Teresin) and shied from speaking about the ugly experiences she had suffered. When she celebrated her 100th birthday two years earlier in 2020, her looks hinted at the beauty she was in her younger years. Her dark hair, obviously dyed, was always styled in a stunning French twist, held by a hand-carved Amber clasp. She wore little make-up, her complexion having hardly been touched by time. Her suits and dresses were often fashioned from the finest of wool Bouclet or of colorful silks that suited her age. In winter, she rarely was seen without her ranch mink with a matching cloche.

Deborah mourned her deeply when she passed away the previous year. Lutz and Deborah often wondered how and why she survived the horrors she must have been subjected to during the two years she was in Teresin. When reading books that awoke ugly memories in Deborah's friend, Henrietta refused to contribute to discussions relating to her personal experiences. It was like she'd made up her mind to keep those times and events buried deep in her subconscious.

✗

This evening, they shared *challah,* the braided loaf of bread, and sweet wine after Deborah blessed these entities, a critical part to the start of the traditional meal. Gefilte fish, and chicken soup with matzo balls, preceded the roasted brisket. The savory kugel was a fine accompaniment to the roasted vegetables. Deborah often served brownies for dessert since she knew Lutz's passion for chocolate. It was the only part of the meal where she broke with tradition.

They finished the meal and Deborah cleared the table. She stashed everything that needed cleaning into the dishwasher at Lutz's insistence. After watching her wash dishes and helping her with the drying for many years, Lutz had been only too happy to succumb to modernity and bought the machine to do the job. Deborah eventually joined him in his study and listened to a performance of Rachmaninoff's Piano Concerto #3 on the radio. The performer was the Ukrainian pianist, Anna Fedorova, playing at The Concertgebouw in Amsterdam.

"That's one of my favorites," Lutz smiled at her.

"Mine, too. She's fabulous and plays with her soul laid bare,"

Deborah said as she sat down pressing her back against the warm tiles of the *Kachelofen* [tiled stove].

Lutz nodded in agreement. His mind was adrift, having been captured momentarily by the piano concert. When Deborah closed her eyes, his turned to focus on Maksyms's manuscript.

※

At Maksym's home it was a different story. Daryna and he were glued to the TV when Maksym's phone alerted him to an incoming call from Ivan using FaceTime.

"Just was in touch with my uncle Bohdan in Kharkiv. The news isn't good. They were shelled heavily and their home flattened. That's bad enough. Far worse, my cousin, Danylo, and their baby were killed. The family is devastated by what's happening," Ivan didn't try to hide his pain.

Maksym saw the tears welling up in Ivan's eyes. "We're so sorry. Helpless is what we are. So close and yet so far. Our hearts reach out to you." He reached for a handkerchief and touched his eyes.

Ivan could hear Maksym's sniffling.

"We have friends in Poland. He's a physician and runs into Ukraine with medical supplies, food, and much-needed things. Most of all he tends to people's medical needs. They also house many of the Ukrainian refugees. Those who are in transit to other neighboring countries and to distant locations receive their help as well. Some have connected with family members living as far away as Canada and the United States. We've collected money here and transferred funds to them. Obviously, there's always more we could do. It's a terrible situation," Maksym said.

"May I change the subject? If I dwell too much on what's happening, I become morose. When we last spoke I became acquainted with your new friend, Dr. Osram. You mentioned meeting him and his twin brother. I had the impression they took a definite interest in your past. Have you learned anything new since that first contact? I suppose, with the start of the war, people have more pressing matters on their minds," Ivan said.

"Lutz and Lenny feel our pain. They've lived in Düsseldorf for most of their lives. They must be in their eighties. Lutz Osram, whom you met via FaceTime, is the one I've seen most frequently. He's a retired professor who taught courses related to literature and writing. He's trying very hard to help with my memoir. What's weird is that I think I look like him. He's an old version of me."

"You're joking?" Ivan wasn't certain if he should share with Maksym what he thought of the strong resemblance the first time he saw the other man's face. His inner voice told him to keep his opinions to himself—at least for now.

"I'm dead serious. Just the other day I saw us in a mirror—side by side. I couldn't believe my eyes. Actually, it scared the hell out of me," Maksym blurted.

"Do you have any idea if and how they might relate to you? You do have somewhat of a challenging history. You never did figure out where you came from and who your forebears were. Sofia and Popov adopted you after you were dumped into their laps by the Giant Shadow. That's what you used to call the character who took you on that long plane ride from Lord knows where. If the situation presents itself, you should consider DNA testing. If Matviyko doesn't want to be part of it, just do it yourself. It could answer a number of questions," Ivan suggested.

"Are you certain? The thought has crossed my mind." He scratched his beard. "I might discover things I'd rather not know."

"And you might learn who you really are and where you came from. There might be an answer to your many nightmares and who the

Giant Shadow was. Who knows? If it was I, nothing would stop me from trying. Just think what doors modern technology could open for you!" Ivan said.

"I'll think about it."

"Let me know what you decide if you pursue DNA. Keep me in the loop. I'm very much interested. It will get me thinking about something other than this damn war." *Sorry, Dad. I know you taught me not to swear.* Ivan looked toward heaven. He often wondered if his father kept an eye on him.

"I'll bring it up again with Lutz when I see him next Wednesday." Maksym exhaled with gusto, then blew his nose not too gently.

Ivan saw the wetness in his eyes.

"Again, I'm still shocked to learn of Danylo's death. And to lose a baby? I feel for his wife and family. I mentioned to you before that we are about to become grandparents, haven't I?"

"You have. How exciting. Have they done any testing to determine the baby's sex?"

"No. They wish it to be a surprise. The attending knows the sex of the child but respects their wishes of not wanting to know. Believing old-wives' tales, Nataliya is almost certain the baby will be a girl. We'll just have to wait and see. We are thrilled to become grandparents at our age." Maksym felt goosebumps just thinking about the prospect of becoming a grandfather for the first time.

"I'm glad you're not that hung up on it being a boy. Our girls certainly have given us much joy," Ivan said. "I share my uncle's pain. It is tragic to lose such a young life."

"He must be devastated. Convey our deepest sympathy. I'll talk with you soon, brother. That's what you are, indeed; you *are* my other brother," Maksym said.

Maksym texted his brother. "Need to talk. Just heard from Ivan."

Matviyko used FaceTime to answer. "What gives, my dear brother. Must be urgent."

"I just connected with Ivan. He had bad news. His uncle Bohdan in Kharkiv lost his son and their baby in an attack on the city. The family is in deep mourning. Ivan feels helpless. They are not allowed to cross into Ukraine from Russian territory. It's all such a waste. What they are doing to our beautiful country is shameful. It will take generations to rebuild if the Ukrainians succeed in keeping their independence," Maksym said. Famous Ukrainian landmarks flashed through his mind.

"You said it. I'm glad we got out of there when we did." Matviyko couldn't resist challenging his brother with unwelcome repartee. He debated if he should ask his next questions. He opened his mouth and went ahead. "What's new with your German friend? Is he still working on your memoir?"

"He is. And he's doing a great job." Maksym opted not to elaborate. There were certain matters he felt more comfortable discussing with Ivan. "I'll let you know when I hear anything new. Have you been in touch with Aunt Sofia? She seems to like where she is, but she misses us."

"That's the impression I have too. I called her after we visited. She liked Lenny and Lutz and said so a couple of times. We should try to see her at least once a month. Think about it. You have a busier schedule than I do. Well, I'll say good night. My eyes are telling me it's time to rest them," Matviyko said.

"Same to you." They signed off simultaneously.

Maksym envisioned Aunt Sofia among the thousands of elderly people fleeing their country and was thankful she was spared the agony. *We made the right decision to flee from Yalta when we did.* He took the last sip of his Cabernet and walked out of his office searching for Daryna. He needed the touch of his loving wife.

He found her bent over some needlework in their den. "Haven't seen you work on that for a long time. What made you pick it up?"

"It's a piece of Hardanger I selected in that Scandinavian gift shop the last time we were in Kyiv. I always loved doing the detail work. I'm bent on finishing it in time for next Christmas. It will be a nice centerpiece under our miniature table tree."

"Who knows where we'll be next Christmas? I'm glad you are so positive with your view of the future," Maksym observed.

When she looked up at him, she saw the tears in his eyes. "Why are you so sad? Did you get bad news?"

"Just talked with Matviyko after speaking with Ivan. Things are pretty bad at home." He told her all he had learned from Ivan. "Things seem to be going from bad to worse."

Daryna reached out, knowing he needed to be close to her. "That makes me very sad. I wonder if we'll ever hear from my family. They are not good at writing and are not into modern communication methods. I'm really worried about them living in the Donbas region. Who knows? They might have been abducted and hauled off to Russia." Daryna shook her head not wanting to believe what she suspected.

Maksym wasn't a praying man. For a split second he beheld Andryi's image before his eyes. Then he bent his knee and made the sign of the cross. Daryna was startled to hear her husband pray the Lord's Prayer in Ukrainian.

Otche nash,	Our Father
shcho yesý na nebesákh,	Which art in heaven,
nekhái sviatýtsia imyá Tvoyé	Hallowed be thy Name.
nekhái pryidé tsárstvo Tvoyé,	Thy Kingdom come.

nekhái budé vólia Tvoyá
yak na nébi,
tak i na zemlí.
Khlib nash nasúshchnyi dai
nam siohódni, i prostý nam
provýny náshi
yak i mý proshcháyemo
vynuváttsiam áshym.
I ne vvedý nas u spokúsu,
alé výzvoly nas vid lukávoho.
Amin

Thy will be done
In earth,
As it is in heaven.
Give us this day our daily bread,
and forgive us our trespasses,
As we forgive those who trespass
against us.
And lead us not into temptation,
But deliver us from evil.
For thine is the kingdom,
The power, and the glory,
Forever and ever. Amen.

Daryna opened the gold-etched Bible she'd brought with her from Yalta. A bookmark took her directly to Psalm 23. Tears running down his cheeks, Maksym joined his wife in the reading.

The LORD is my shepherd; I shall not want.

He maketh me to lie down in green pastures: he leadeth me beside the still waters.

He restoreth my soul: he leadeth me in the paths of righteousness for his name's sake.

Yea, though I walk through the valley of the shadow of death, I will fear no evil: for thou art with me; thy rod and thy staff they comfort me.

Thou preparest a table before me in the presence of mine enemies: thou anointest my head with oil; my cup runneth over.

Surely goodness and mercy shall follow me all the days of my life: and I will dwell in the house of the LORD forever.

When he raised his eyes, he smiled at Daryna. "Andryi taught us well. I know he would be proud. Sorry to say, I can't recall the last time I prayed or set foot in a church. But, after all that is happening right now, I believe the time has come for me to make some changes."

Chapter 17

MAKSYM was anxious. He couldn't wait to see Lutz after their last visit. That image in the mirror haunted him day and night. *Why hadn't I seen that before?* He rushed up the steps and halted for a moment to catch his breath before pressing the button. For the first time he noticed the ornate, oblong object next to the doorbell, appearing to point toward the opening into the house. *Wonder what that is? Have to ask Lutz about its meaning and purpose.*

Lutz was expecting his weekly visitor by two o'clock. When he heard the musical chimes, he rose from his chair to answer the call. Lutz couldn't help feeling the quaking in his knees. He bent to touch his left which talked to him lately. *Maybe I should listen to Deborah and have it replaced one of these days. Dammit! It's hell to get old.*

On Wednesday afternoons, Deborah still met with several ladies at their book club. Lutz and Maksym had the house to themselves and could talk without interruptions. Lutz opened the door and held his breath for a second. His right hand clutched his chest.

"What have you done?" Lutz was stunned to see Maksym clean-shaven. "You've relinquished your Jewish visage. Deep down I envied that beard of yours. I never could grow decent facial hair." He reached to shake Maksym's hand and didn't know what possessed him. He moved close to the younger man and hugged him firmly.

When Lutz leaned into him, Maksym thought he was about to kiss him.

Lutz smiled toward the Almighty. Finally, he'd seen what he wanted to see. His eyes glistened as he released Maksym at last.

"What was that all about? I hope I didn't work up a sweat. My deodorant must still be doing its job." He pretended taking a whiff from his armpits. "What's with the tears in your eyes?"

Lutz just smiled and ignored the question.

"I wasn't sure how to interpret your expression of emotion. All I shed was my beard, not my virginity. Daryna became tired of going to bed with Santa Claus. She joked that I'd become more German than Germans are. Shaving off the white whiskers after a few years was her idea, and now, when I look at my naked face, I have to agree with her. I didn't just lose my beard. I lost a few years."

Lutz had joy in his voice. "You didn't lose anything. You've gained your youth." *And much more.* He didn't want to make any other comments. Lutz knew what would happen next in their journey toward the ultimate resurrection.

"Isn't it great that men can hug and shed tears? I remember when such gentle behavior between men was viewed by most in our society as *verboten*," Lutz said as they walked toward his office.

Maksym couldn't help noticing the slight limp in Lutz's gait. "You can say that again. Andryi let us in on that secret. He had no problem being affectionate with anyone. In Popov's world, we never came closer to boys and men than shaking hands. He would have beaten the shit out of us had he ever seen us hug a male. I don't know how often he slapped me when he caught me shedding a tear, no matter how hard I tried to hide my feelings."

"That's so sad."

They sat down in familiar chairs and looked at each other. Maksym spotted a sculpture gracing the wall behind Lutz, a magnificent depiction of a tree of life. "That's a beautiful piece. Strange, I didn't notice it before. It isn't new, is it?" Maksym asked. He wondered if he was losing it, making two new discoveries in one day. *My mind must have been on other things.*

Lutz saw the questioning expression on Maksym's face that was followed by the shrugging of his shoulders. "Oh no. It's been in my office for quite a while. As a matter of fact, Deborah bought it for our twenty-fifth anniversary. It's a wonderful way of tracing one's ancestry. Something that, unfortunately, will never be of interest to anyone in our lives," Lutz said.

"How so?"

"I didn't produce any children, and neither did Lenny."

That comment struck Maksym. *Then, where did Matviyko and I come from if they didn't have any children? Ivan may be right. DNA ancestry is a good idea and may shed light on who Matviyko and I are.* He looked back at Lutz and focused on the old man's face.

"My sister and her family have vanished. Who will give a damn after we're gone? Ancestry is significant to me as a practicing Jew. You've heard me say that part of our heritage was stolen from us when the Nazis destroyed our synagogues on *Kristallnacht on November 9,* 1938. Then they took my father and murdered him in 1943. I was just a young boy, but when I thought about it later as I grew into manhood, it made me angry to think about what Hitler tried to do. He attempted to eradicate our past and present and preclude us from having a future." There was that moistness again in Lutz's eyes. "Forgive my emotional reactions."

Maksym faced Lutz. "I must confess something. The last time I saw you and had you hold onto me after you were momentarily unsteady on your feet, I glanced at the two of us in that full-length mirror as we approached the foyer. Then, honest to God, I thought you were my long-lost father." Maksym looked into those dark eyes across the vast rosewood desk. They were blinking away the sadness with practiced subtlety.

For a second, Lutz was tempted to reveal what he believed to be the truth. "It's strange you saying that. I had that feeling of knowing you from the moment we first met weeks ago at *Im Goldenen Kessel*. But, of course, I learned long ago that we humans are related somewhere, somehow. If you believe in that sort of thing, we are all descendants of Adam and Eve."

"True, very true," Maksym nodded. "I'm making all sorts of new discoveries." *Could their long-lost sister have been our mother?* Maksym opted to be patient, not letting his thoughts interrupt the flow of their conversation. "I noticed the pretty encasing with Hebrew inscriptions next to the doorbell. Would you share with me what is its purpose or meaning?"

Lutz smiled. *Maybe somewhere in your subconscious you are beginning to realize that you're part of the Jewish tribe.* "You *are* inquisitive today. It's a *mezuzah.* It houses a parchment inscribed in black indelible ink with verses from the Torah. The prayer begins with *Shema Yisrael* [Hear, O Israel, the Lord (is) our God, the Lord is One.] Jews believe that the *mezuzah* repels evil from crossing their threshold. Orthodox Jews may have *mezuzot* at every doorway to rooms other than bathrooms. We usually touch it, showing respect to God, and kiss our finger after touching the *mezuzah.*"

"It reminds me of the *Hand of Fatima* or *Khamsa* one sees at doorways of Muslim homes in the Middle East. We learned of its significance while visiting Morocco," Maksym responded.

"That's correct. It's become a symbol of peace between Muslims and Jews living in that region. And speaking of peace, what's happening with family and friends in Ukraine?" Lutz asked.

"My close friend, Ivan, lost family in Kharkiv. Even a newborn was killed. They are in total shock. We are all so helpless although we try to do what we can to make certain things possible financially. But even if Ivan wanted to, he's not allowed to cross over into Ukraine from Yalta."

"I can't stand watching the news on TV and seeing what that butcher is doing to your people and your beautiful country. He's a madman for certain. We've traveled to Ukraine. I've never forgotten seeing *Andrea Chenier* at the beautiful opera house in Odessa. Most of us never heard of a city called Mariupol. Now it dominates the front pages and comparisons are drawn to Aleppo, Guernica, and Leningrad. I hear of people hoarding flour and oil, and the prices of heating fuel and benzine are going through the roof," Lutz said, wishing he could change the subject.

"Friends of mine complained, having paid four times more for their heating oil than they did a year ago. But, of course, keeping things in perspective, we should count our blessings," Maksym responded.

"Sad, sad. For me it's déjà vu. I never thought I would see another world war start in Europe after the last warmongering leaders were defeated in 1945. Guess there will always be another one to challenge humanity. Just think of all the other wars the world has seen since 1945."

Maksym faced Lutz, wishing to avoid further discussion of the present situation. "Do you go to temple regularly?"

"Yes. These days I attend services every Saturday at the Leo Baeck Saal. It's the new synagogue that opened in 1958. After it was bombed by two fanatics in 2000, the temple is under constant watch by the police." He took a sip from his glass. Lutz for once listened to Deborah's reminder to stay hydrated. He hated drinking plain water.

In that respect he was like many Germans who often joked that consuming gobs of water did nothing but rust one's pipes.

"As a Reform Jew, I don't attend temple every day, but Deborah and I keep *Shabbat* every Friday night and honor certain special days throughout the year. It's become our tradition. It makes me feel connected to my ancestors." Without consulting with Maksym, Lutz poured them a cognac and lifted his glass. "*L'Chaim*! To life! Let's you and I talk about something more pleasant."

"What might that be? My memoir? Do I dare ask?"

"Your memoir is doing just fine. You may need to add some chapters before we're done. But, there's something much more current I want to discuss."

Maksym looked puzzled. "What did you have in mind?"

"Have you or Matviyko ever attended a Jewish Seder celebration? Passover or Pesach starts on the 15th of April this year. It's next week on Friday after sundown. Lenny has a huge dining room." *He thought of having the meal. You're fibbing, Lutz.* He faced Maksym and continued. "While he isn't a practicing Jew, he wants to do this. Since Anna passed away, he needs to be close to family." While the latter was true, Lutz knew he was telling tales, but there was no need to confuse Maksym.

"I've never experienced a Seder. I don't believe Matviyko has either."

"Deborah and I would like to have all of you in your close circle be part of the traditional Pesach meal." Lutz looked for a response from his visitor.

Maksym seemed stunned. "That's quite a few people. Actually, we are talking about at least nine. It includes Matviyko and his significant other, Julia, Ivan's sister, Varida, her friend, Walter, myself, Daryna, our daughter, Nataliya, her husband, Anton, and, of course,

Aunt Sofia. I'm sure she would love the change of wallpaper and want to be part of this gathering," Maksym kept counting his fingers.

"There's no issue. One of you young men could fetch Aunt Sofia. If you don't have a way of accommodating her, she could overnight with us. There's no problem that I can see," Lutz added.

"Holy crap, Lutz, I haven't been called a young man in years. It sounds great. Although, before we get too carried away with this family gathering, I have one more far-fetched request. I discussed it with Ivan after my mirror revelation last week. Would you have a problem with doing a DNA test? It's been suggested to us on several occasions. But I believe I'm ready to explore it at this time."

"No, not at all. It has crossed my mind." Lutz turned his head for a second not wanting to convey any signals of duplicity. *Should have thought of that a long time ago.*

"Matviyko is frequently involved with individuals pursuing paternity suits. When we discussed the chance of doing this, he advised me that he had no interest in participating but urged me to have a witness present if and when we collect samples and that specimens are properly labeled."

Lutz was aware of German laws pertaining to the protocols involved. "Matviyko is absolutely correct. Let me call my neighbor, Martin. I can't believe the convenience; he happens to work for a lab that processes DNA kits. He's shared with Lenny and me some stories he's heard. So many people are willing to pay good money for the magic bullet only to discover things they wish had remained in the closet. He'll be happy to oblige. One of his favorite beers in the fridge will be sufficient reward for him."

Forty-five minutes later the swabs taken by Martin were securely ensconced in the application kits he'd provided. Forms were duly executed and witnessed. Then, at Martin's suggestion, Maksym whipped out his trusty phone and registered Lutz and himself with "MyHeritage DNA" online. He opted for the "Ancestry plus Traits" package at €99 each. Martin was given sufficient money to process the kits for expedited services.

After his earlier discovery, Lutz thought it was a waste of money. Still, he was willing to go along with Maksym's quest for verification. He didn't dream of breathing a word.

Martin enjoyed his second beer and was only too willing to oblige his elderly neighbor. He kept studying Lutz's mien. It hadn't been more than a few minutes into the process that Martin realized Lutz was merely going along to please the younger man. Just reading their faces, he had no doubt they were related although he continued to be puzzled by the names of Osram and Popov. He decided not to go there but hoped he'd hear the rest of the story when the results were returned.

Maksym checked his watch and realized he'd perhaps overstayed his visit. It was past six o'clock when he rose to leave. "It sure stays light with daylight savings time. I don't know where the afternoon went."

"Deborah's book club must have run late, too," Lutz noted.

"How about I do not bother you next Wednesday since the family and I will see you at the Seder on Friday?" Maksym asked.

"That's completely up to you. If you want to show, I'll be here." Lutz got up, pushing himself out of the deep chair with the help of both arms. Sitting for long stretches did reveal the impact of aging. He held onto Maksym as they walked toward the mirror in the foyer. Both smiled as they beheld their images.

Lutz opened his arms, wanting to embrace the younger man. He thought, he better not—but he didn't want to let go.

Maksym had inclinations to do the same but thought it was best to just walk away after shaking hands. First, he had to clear his head.

Lutz closed the front door with deliberation after he'd raised his right hand to wave goodbye to Maksym. He turned toward his office and noticed that the chestnut tree was resplendent in green and fully leafed out. The leaves touching his windows, barely moved by a gentle breeze, were kinder than the naked branches in the depth of winter. He looked forward to May and never tired of seeing the colorful spectacle, his eyes delighted by the multitude of pink candelabras, the flowers of chestnut trees in bloom.

The grandfather clock struck the half-hour past six o'clock. Still, there was no sign of Deborah. Lutz stopped walking for a moment and then refreshed his cognac snifter before sitting in the red wingback where Maksym had sat. The leather still conveyed the warmth of its previous occupant. Lutz gently touched the worn leather. After he took another sip of his drink, he closed his eyes and sighed. "*Schicksal,*" [fate] was all he said. He smiled, remembering what one of his contemporaries had told him earlier in the day. "Lutz, it's better to be seen than to be viewed."

He debated refreshing his drink. His mind was in an uproar. *What if?* He wondered. He didn't know what brought on his search for explanations. Was it pure sentimentality? A function of his age? *What if Fernando hadn't taken Doretta and the older children on that trip to Antarctica? What if that Giant Shadow hadn't come along and stolen those boys? They would never have become Ukrainians and by a stroke of fate would never have landed in Düsseldorf. They would never have known a different culture and pursued educational paths that led them to where they are now. They might have become vintners. My God, had they not been abducted and left to fend for themselves in Yalta, they might have been killed along with Fernando, Doretta, Mario, and Alona during that uprising in Chile in September 1973. Perhaps, ironically, the Giant Shadow saved their lives? Yes, he saved their lives by stealing them, but he set them on a path no one had ever dreamed of. What if they hadn't fled Yalta, they might have become victims of anti-Semitism again pervading under Russian influence. What if Lenny hadn't spotted them at Im Goldenen Kessel on that chilly night in February? What if the strong resemblance hadn't registered in his mind? We would never have known of their existence.*

Lutz enjoyed the warmth of cognac sliding down his throat. *Serendipity! Most of our lives are shaped by its influence. Had Hektor Birken not jilted my sister, she would never have moved to Zürich and eventually met and married Fernando Garcia López. Had it not been for Andreas, Mom's second husband, dying on the plane as they were returning from Chile, Doretta wouldn't have come to be with Mother. It was during that short visit we got to know each other better. We had not seen each other in years. Doretta and I discovered the strength of our link to the Jewish father we hardly knew before he was torn from our lives.*

A draft caused by the opening of the front door caught his attention. Lutz hadn't heard the key turn. When he looked up, he was pleased to see Deborah walk into his office. "Must have been an exciting discussion with your lady friends," Lutz greeted her.

"None of us could stop talking about the latest thriller by Louise Penny, "State of Terror," which she co-authored with no other than Hillary Rodham Clinton. The book is eye-opening and frightening. It's all about the umbrella of fear we are experiencing at this very moment. A world in disgrace. None of us was able to stop the discussion. You should read it. You will not enjoy it but you won't be able to put it down." She could tell he was off in some other hemisphere, not listening to her blabbering. "How was your afternoon with Maksym?"

"I have no questions left in my mind. He is Elijah Avraham, the firstborn of the twins. He shaved off his beard, and I could see the birthmark. Maksym and Matviyko are our long-lost nephews. I've been sitting here for the last hour or so, "what-ifing." It's amazing what conclusions I arrived at. Had they not been abducted, our lives would have been differently affected. *Schicksal!* That's all I can say. Sit down. Let's talk for a while. We'll go across the street and have a bite a little later. Care to join me for a drink?"

"Why not? Surprise me!"

When he returned from the bar, he couldn't help chuckling. "Here's your favorite poison. I still know how to make a mean Rusty Nail."

"Yes you do! And you still know how to charm yourself into my heart. I'm so glad the Almighty has been kind, allowing us to enjoy this time together. I'm pleased you unearthed this strong link to Doretta; I've always known how much you missed her." She saw him pressing his knuckles into his eyes. "Tell me what happened?"

"I was so shocked when Maksym showed up all clean-shaven, and I knew instantly what I had to do. No question about it, I took him by total surprise when I hugged him. It wasn't just about my need to confirm the presence of the birthmark; I wanted to be close to him. After discovering our resemblance as he left the last time, he had similar feelings toward me."

"That impromptu embrace of yours was almost like a Judas kiss. Did you at least let him know what it was all about?"

"I was tempted but decided against it. When he approached me again about having DNA testing, I didn't want to disillusion him. I knew Lenny had much more convincing evidence of the boys, as Sofia still insists on calling Maksym and Matviyko. According to the book, Martin came over and processed all that DNA stuff. It's now floating somewhere in Cyberspace and in the trusted care of the German postal system. Lord knows when we shall hear."

"You aren't kidding. Too bad they couldn't handle everything over the internet."

"True, true. Good old Martin didn't say a word. He went along with sampling saliva, completing lengthy questionnaires, and getting everything signed, sealed, and delivered. He knew, as did I, that Maksym was wasting more than two-hundred euro."

"So how did you leave it as he departed today? Don't keep me in the dark."

"I have this strong desire to create in them a need to know more about their heritage, in particular their link to Judaism. Let's face it, Doretta didn't choose their names by drawing them from a hat. She wanted to honor our father and the faith that cost Father his life."

"That's admirable on your part. You have a plan?"

"As a matter of fact, I do. Both Lenny and you will play a major part. I advised Maksym that you and I are giving a Pesach Seder at Lenny's house."

"How could you?"

"How could I not? Things happened so quickly. I needed to act fast. Maksym bought it and is the one who will invite the other eight to the meal. Of course, Lenny will be shocked at first, but in good time, he'll see the light and what I'm planning to stage with his and your help. He told me he's pretty much set with the PowerPoint presentation. He discovered a regular treasure trove behind those louvered shutters in his office."

"What about preparations? Who will do the shopping and the cooking?"

"*Die Kurve* will take care of most of the catering. More importantly, I want you to arrange a day or two of major cleaning with Ulrike Nötig starting on April 13. I will gladly foot the bill if he gives us any hassle about paying her. It will be worth every *Pfennig*."

"I'm impressed. You thought of everything."

"Glad you think so; this legal noggin can still process a case. However, there are certain things in life one never forgets. It's like riding a bicycle or being a *Düsseldorfer Radschläger.*"

"I haven't seen you do either in many a year and do me a big favor; please, don't try." She couldn't stop laughing. "I can just see it."

"I might surprise you," Lutz grinned.

"Spare me the agony. The 'Nail' hit the spot. Now, take me out for a bite. All this talk about feasting and celebrating made me hungry." She extended her right hand, offering to assist him in getting out of the red wingback.

Lutz had no intention of declining the offer. Once balanced on his two feet, he bowed graciously toward his fair lady. "It's good to be seen and better than being viewed!" Lutz chuckled.

Deborah cracked up. "Where did that originate?"

"Ferdinand mentioned it this morning when we were discussing the aches and pains of aging. Like you, I almost lost it. Ferdinand is damn right!"

Lutz held her black Merino wrap and then opened the front door. The short walk to *Restaurant da Noi* was refreshing. Entering the place, Deborah smiled. "Just what I felt like. Nothing beats a good Italian dinner. I'll let you make a choice while I go and powder my nose."

He rubbed his stomach, placing the sizable red napkin in his lap as he inhaled unmistakable fragrances, promising the delights of Italian cuisine. He glanced up at the waiter who proclaimed the evening's specials in an Italianate-accented voice. Lutz was sure he'd made the right choice.

As Deborah approached their table, she spotted Lutz's attempt at rising from his chair. "Don't be a fool trying to still be my gentleman.

Those chairs don't look all that sturdy. That's all I would need having you fall and break a hip."

"Thanks for being so insightful. I am getting to be an oldie these days. Of course, Grandma taught us well." He caught the waiter's attention. "Have the bartender fix us a couple of Rob Roys. Up! He does a great job on those. We'll enjoy them while looking over the menu."

"Will do." He was back with their libations shortly.

Lutz raised his glass toward the light. He loved the color blinking through the crystal goblet. "Here's to the end of a perfect day. L'Chaim. I've loved my life with you. Let's discover what the rest of our days have to offer." They set down their glasses. Lutz reached across the table and touched Deborah's hands—she was obviously moved by the warmth of connecting.

"Thank you, my chevalier. I too am looking forward to exciting discoveries," Deborah winked at Lutz.

Chapter 18

THE phone rang in Frankfurt. Maksym wanted to contact Ivan's sister, Varida. Her lover, Walter, looked at the incoming call and recognized the name. "Varida, there's a call from Maksym Popov. I'm sure you want to take it. I know you said earlier you didn't want any interruptions, but this caller is special to you."

"You're so right." She took the phone from Walter's hand and stretched out on a large leather sofa, wriggling her toes, trying to shed her slippers. "What a nice surprise. I hope your call doesn't mean more bad news from home. Lately I'm frightened to pick up the blasted thing."

"I understand. Relax, girl, this is good news and a special request. I would really appreciate it if you and Walter could see your way clear to spend Friday evening, April 15 in Düsseldorf. You and our families, as well as Aunt Sofia, have been invited to participate in a Passover Seder at the home of some dear people with whom we have recently become acquainted. They want this to be a family affair and are including us to take our minds off what's happening daily in the homeland. They know about Danylo and the baby and feel terrible.

Aside from that, it's been too long since we've been together. What do you say?" Maksym pleaded.

She covered the phone. "Jewish friends of Maksym's have invited us to their home for a Passover celebration. It's at night a week from Friday. I would like to go. Are you game to join me? He needs to know. We could stay overnight and spend a little time with Matviyko. I've never met his significant other. It's been an eternity since we last saw Matviyko or Maksym and his family. If you remember, we didn't make it to Nataliya's wedding. Perhaps you don't recall, she and Anton wrote the nicest thank you letter."

Walter nodded affirmatively. Varida brushed one of her hairs off the phone. "Tell your friends we'll be there for sure. Don't bother with fetching us at the train station. We'll take a cab and probably get there late afternoon. I presume you're still at the same address and haven't moved into an old folks home in the meantime?"

"You must be joking. Never. Besides that, we aren't that old. Daryna loves the place, She made it our home."

"Can't wait to see you. Hi to Matviyko. Is he still seeing the same woman? Wasn't her name Julia?" Varida asked.

"Yes. I wish he'd marry her," Maksym said.

"Oh, you and your old-fashioned conventions. You're just like Dad. He's probably turning in his grave, knowing I've been living in sin. Who cares about that little bit of paper? Not I." She took a healthy sip from her cocktail glass. "Love ya. See you next week."

Varida had left him speechless. The way she slurred her words, Maksym was sure she was at least on her third round. He was confident the following three calls would be easier. When he reached Aunt Sofia, she was surprised at first and then utterly delighted to accept the invitation to spend the evening in the presence of "her boys" and their families. When she heard where the party was to be held and the occasion for the gathering, she was taken off guard but thought she'd better not refuse the invitation. Then Aunt Sofia suddenly recalled the thoughts that originally crossed her mind when she first met Lutz and Lenny. She just knew there was a connection between those four men. But no matter what, the chance to be with Maksym and Matviyko again sealed the deal.

Julia, Matviyko's partner, was excited to meet new and different people and spend time with Maksym and his family. There were times when she was downright jealous of Daryna. She assured Maksym that there would be no problem with picking up Aunt Sofia in Kaiserswerth.

Wanting to speak to his daughter, Maksym saved the easiest for last. He touched the FaceTime app for Nataliya. Anton, his son-in-law, picked up her phone. "Hallo, Papa. How nice of you to check on us. Is everything okay in your bailiwick?" he asked.

"Everything is just fine and dandy at this place. But, more importantly, how's Nataliya doing with her pregnancy?"

"We are counting the days, but she's doing well. Don't mention it to Nataliya, but she's beginning to look like a whale. She wouldn't be too happy if she heard me say that. We put the final touches on the nursery the other day. Dr. Braun told us it could happen any moment now and that we might be in for a surprise. Neither Nataliya nor I were quite sure how to interpret his strange remark. Guess it was our decision not to know the sex of the new arrival."

Maksym couldn't help smiling. "We can't wait to hold our first grandchild in our arms. But I'm calling about something more imminent. Are you two by chance not booked for Friday night, the 15th? I know how busy a social life you usually lead on weekends. Our whole family has been invited to a Passover Seder by our Jewish friends."

There was a pregnant pause. Anton walked into their library

where Nataliya was grading papers. She was seated in his comfortable leather chair, her feet resting on the glass-covered desktop. He hesitated for a second and then shared her father's request with her.

She looked puzzled as well and reached for the cell. "Hi Dad. Is this for real? How often do Jewish people invite Christians to a Seder?"

"As far as I know, they are not orthodox, and it has nothing to do with religion. They learned of Uncle Ivan's terrible losses and want to do something meaningful for our whole Ukrainian family in the diaspora. There's really no better explanation I can give you. They're just being nice."

"I've never been to a Seder. What's it like, do you know?"

"I don't know all the details, but we'll find out."

"Is there anything we should bring?"

"Good question. I doubt it. Ask some of your Jewish colleagues."

A frown crowned her forehead. "I'm sad to learn of Uncle Ivan's losses. But, of course, Anton and I will be there. Please convey our sympathies when you speak to him. I wish you'd let me know right away; I would have texted him."

"Sorry. I had too many other things on my brain." Maksym shook his head. "Make a note on your calendar. It's shortly after sundown, right around 8:30, on Friday, April 15." He was aware that at this late stage in her pregnancy it might slip Nataliya's mind.

Nataliya entered the exact time and place into her phone.

"By the way, Aunt Varida and Walter will also be coming. You haven't seen each other in years."

"That's great, Dad. After they didn't show up at our wedding, I wondered if we'd ever see them again. We are so much looking forward to the event next Friday." She ended the call and raised her shoulders as she faced Anton. "I just hope this little bundle of joy doesn't decide to emerge at an inconvenient point in time." She touched her protruding abdomen with a gentle hand. She often was puzzled by the baby's strange heartbeat.

Maksym poured himself a stiff drink. He believed he deserved to celebrate. He couldn't wait to share with Daryna the events of the day. He found her sitting in a rocker in her sewing room engrossed in a magazine. "Care for a drink?" He took a sip of his cognac. "I sure needed that one." He smacked his lips.

"Don't mind if I do. You can pour me a real short one."

He handed Daryna the crystal snifter and lifted his glass. "L'Chaim! L'Chaim, indeed." He had forgotten where he had heard that toast before.

Chapter 19

HAVING rested well, Lutz craved his first cup of coffee. His flannel pajamas and fleece-lined slippers felt especially comfortable this morning as he walked toward his office. He barely noticed the grandfather clock and wasn't sure if it had dinged eight or nine times. A quick glance at his phone confirmed that it was just after eight. *Of course, I'll probably piss him off by calling so early. But then, I have important matters to convey.*

Seated at his desk, he was confident he'd have all the information he needed to enlighten Lenny about the upcoming event. Lutz could see it all happen. Finally, the mystery of the abducted nephews would be solved and the truth revealed of what happened fifty-one years ago. He touched the FaceTime app and faced his brother in an instant.

"Hope you had a good night. We need to talk."

"Oh, I know what that means. Usually, you confront me with fait accompli actions over which I have little control. Damn! Sometimes you scare the shit out of me. What is it this time, my trusted legal counselor?" Lenny couldn't hide a smirk crossing his face.

"How well you know me. Things with Maksym went into overdrive yesterday, and I had to act fast."

"Okay, let me have it." A noisy yawn underscored his last statement. Lenny was now all ears.

"You are having eleven guests for a Pesach Seder at your house on Friday the 15th, starting at 8:30. Sunset is at 8:29."

"You're joking, aren't you?" Lenny threw his arms in the air. His face expressed total disbelief.

"Not at all. The only thing you need to do is to have that Power-Point production ready for a showing after dinner. We'll take care of the rest. Our cleaning lady will be at your place as long as is necessary on the 13th. Her name is Ulrike Nötig. She'll get there by nine in the morning. Then, if need be, she'll finish on the 14th. Had I been certain you'd have your ass out of bed by the time the birds started singing, I'd have told her to get there at eight. But since I know you've become an owl in your old age, I didn't dare sic her on you that early in the morning."

Lenny ignored his brother's drivel as he had labeled Lutz's commentary on occasion. Still, the name of the cleaning lady had caught his attention. "How ironic. Is that really her name? *Nötig?* [necessary]. You're shitting me?"

"No, Lenny. I believe it's her brand name, but we've never known her by any other," Lutz said.

"But what about all the other stuff that's involved?"

"Deborah will make some contributions and arrange the table. We're getting the bulk of the meal from *Die Kurve*—an excellent kosher and Middle Eastern restaurant and caterer. We've used them before."

"Sounds like you've thought of everything."

"Almost. I couldn't do it alone. However, it's that legal mind of mine that's still firing on all cylinders." He laughed out loud.

"Mind telling me who my honored guests might be?"

"The ones coming the furthest are Varida and her partner, Walter, who live in Frankfurt and will lodge with Maksym. Varida is the sister of Ivan, Maksym's closest friend who's still a practicing ob/gyn in Yalta. Varida and Walter will be taking the train. She offered to take a cab to Maksym's place. Matviyko and his gal, Julia, will pick up Aunt Sofia at Kaiserswerth. Maksym and his wife, Daryna, their daughter, Nataliya, and her husband, Anton, round out their contingent. Of course, I'm bringing Deborah along. And you are the honored host."

Lenny added up the number of guests in his head. "Glad that my dining room table can seat twelve comfortably. I gather that was your plan. Care to share any other significant information with me? For example, what might have triggered this elaborate party to be staged at my home?"

"Let me say that confirmation of what we suspected might arrive just in time from "MyHeritage DNA"—the DNA analysts of renown. Does that give you enough of a clue?"

"Gotcha," was all Lenny could say.

"Make sure you include all the slides that our brother-in-law, Fernando, and nephew, Mario, took from the time when Elijah and Eduardo were born until they disappeared. It should make for enlightening after-dinner conversation. But I really don't expect any surprises. Do you?" Lutz asked.

"Not really. It's all there in somewhat-faded Technicolor. Thanks for sharing Frau Nötig with me. The place can stand a good hauling over. Believe me, it needs more than a lick and a promise. But now that I think about it, I need to confess. I'm quite excited and look forward to the evening."

"I knew you would see it my way. Deborah and I thank you for opening your home. If you hadn't accepted your part as graciously as you have, I would have reminded you that you were the one who opened Pandora's Box."

"Guess I'll never live that one down but what an interesting box it will be when we get to the bottom. Thanks for making all the arrangements. I couldn't have done it in such short order."

"Yes, you could've. You never lost your touch when it came to closing a deal." Lutz grinned at his brother.

"Now you've really done it."

Lenny touched the end button and sighed. He walked to the kitchen and headed for his coffee brewer. In his mind, the slides and videos he had assembled flashed before his eyes. He still couldn't believe that he and his brother were about to shine a light on an unsolved crime. He only wished their beloved sister, Doretta, had lived to see the day. How he longed to touch her and connect with her and her family in Chile to share the good news. Lenny knew he was reaching for the moon and was glad no one saw the tears.

He bent to pick up the photograph in its hammered, heavy silver frame sitting on an ebony side table beside his well-worn leather recliner. It was the photo his beloved Anna had taken of Doretta, Lutz, and himself. Its vibrant colors were bleached by the passing of fifty years. Yet, the image that captured the Osram siblings in the prime of their lives would never fade from his visual memory. He recalled how jealous he was of the close relationship he'd observed between Doretta and Lutz, its foundation their faith and shared memories of their father, who'd been slaughtered by the Nazis. It was the last time the siblings connected. Doretta had made the long trip from Santiago, Chile, because she felt a need to be with her family after her mother was suddenly widowed for a second time. Only a year had passed since the twins were abducted. A year later Doretta and her entire family vanished, never to be heard from again.

Lenny set down the photo. *What a fool I was not to marry you, Anna.* He searched for his handkerchief, hiding in his pajama pants, and wiped his eyes. If it wasn't so early in the day, he would have doused his coffee with *Asbach Uralt,* the German answer to cognac. But instead he commandeered Alexa to activate the TV.

As much as he hated it, he needed to know what was happening in Ukraine. He was tempted to reach for a cigar safely ensconced in the silver-embossed humidor on his desk. He shook his head. *I better keep in mind what Dr. Hollander told me.*

Chapter 20

Lenny strolled through the house and was pleased with Ulrike Nötig's efforts to make his home presentable to the invited guests. Deborah succeeded in creating a masterpiece of a dining room table. He glanced at the sterling silver flatware that had not graced his table since Anna's death. Frau Nötig did a fine job polishing all the silver in the house. His sister-in-law chose his favorite pattern, the Meissen Blue Onion, from among the collections of fine china Anna had acquired successfully through the years. He ran a finger across a bare end table double-checking on the absence of dust. He grinned. *Good job!*

"You didn't trust Ulrike? She's worth every Euro you spent. Glad you're pleased with her work and the table. Are you all set with your PowerPoint presentation?" Deborah asked.

"Indeed. I'm as ready as I can be. Why did you take down the screen?" Lenny asked.

"It didn't add to the dining room while we enjoyed the Seder. Also, I didn't want the caterers tripping over the legs of the equipment. Lutz will help you get the screen set when the time comes."

"Okay. I can buy that argument. When are you expecting the catering service to show?"

"They wanted to set up shortly after seven and will be ready to serve after *Kiddush. So* I will start the service but Lutz will say the blessing and serve the wines. He might even sing; his voice is still tolerable."

"True. I never could carry a tune. I was much better at operating calculators. Before I fail to mention it, those floral arrangements you did are outstanding." He ran his right hand lovingly across the tops of the blooms.

"Don't say a word about it. Lutz will surely comment that for once he got his money's worth having paid dearly for my lessons in floral arranging. He thinks you're a tightwad. He's just as bad. I thought the dwarf spring flowers made for colorful arrangements that were low enough not to interfere with the flow of the conversation. I will light the candles after the guests are seated. I believe none outside our family are of the Jewish faith."

"You're correct. Of course, after our little show, Maksym and Matviyko will join our ranks. I gather their company from Frankfurt has arrived?"

"Yes. Maksym called and said Varida's taking a nap, and Walter is filling him in on the latest they heard from Ivan. The situation in Ukraine is becoming desperate. What's happening to those poor souls in Mariupol is particularly frightening. Hundreds, perhaps thousands, are hiding under that steel plant without necessary food, drink, or medical supplies. Corpses are rotting away in the shelter and the living conditions are unbearable. Who knows how it all will end." Deborah was close to tears. She reached for the trailing hem of her apron.

Lenny took his sister-in-law in his arms. "Now, there, there." He lifted up her chin. "I'm glad we have something uplifting planned for the evening. It will be good for all present. Is it presumptuous of me to inquire about the planned menu for tonight? I know there will be an abundance of matzoh."

Deborah was thankful for Lenny's attempt at changing the topic. "The staff from *Die Kurve* will prepare three Seder plates consisting of roasted egg, horseradish for the bitter herb, lettuce, shank bone, pieces of apple, nuts, and spices, as well as parsley—all elements of remembering the Exodus story. I assume your brother will lead the ceremony.

"Of course, there will be the washing of hands before we partake of the various parts of the Seder plate, especially in this era of the Covid virus. Appropriate wines will be served during the ceremony.

"During the main part of the meal, we'll sample gefilte fish, matzoh ball soup, and roasted lamb. *Die Kurve* does a great job on the main dishes. We won't be hiding the larger part of a broken matzoh, the *afikomen,* since no young children are in attendance seeking to locate the hiding place."

"I never realized my brother became so deeply involved with Judaic practices over the last fifty years. He never made any attempts at pros- elytizing or urging me to convert. I'm not much of a Catholic either. Grandma would be terribly disappointed in me. I can't remember the last time I set foot in a church."

"Don't tell your brother. He won't give you peace until you grace a church or temple entrance. Certainly, he'd never meet you for a beer on a Friday night. *Shabbat* is a vital part of his life."

She checked the table once more when the doorbell rang. "Sounds like our first guests have arrived," Deborah said as she walked across the Asian runner to the front door. She was pleased to see what an excellent job Frau Nötig had done in refreshing all of Lenny's fabulous rugs. She was almost certain the woman had done the *Sauerkraut* treatment. It always brought the colors in the carpets to life.

It was Maksym and his entourage. He introduced their friend, Varida, and her partner, Walter, and then his wife, daughter and son-in-law. Maksym announced with much pride that they were expectant grandparents. Maksym and Daryna presented their host with a large Rosenthal bowl holding a fine collection of sweets and Pesach-appropriate wines. There was hand-shaking all around. Lenny smiled. He was pleased to be hosting the party.

Next to ring the doorbell was Matviyko. Julia held tightly onto Aunt Sofia. There were expressions of joy all around. As Aunt Sofia embraced Lutz, she whispered in his ear: "Thank you for leading my boys back home." There was that all-knowing mysterious smile on her face.

Deborah called attention to place cards. Lutz and Lenny would sit at each end of the table. Deborah's place was on Lutz's right, and Aunt Sofia was to his left. Maksym and his family were seated next to Aunt Sofia. Across the table sat Walter and Varida and Matviyko and Julia. Lenny was pleased that Nataliya and Julia were his conversationalists.

The last rays of the sun sank beneath the horizon. Looking out the large windows, they beheld clouds tinged in yellow, orange, mauve, and a touch of purple marking the end of the day. The dinner conversation was lively until Deborah stood to light the candles in *Shabbat* manner. She spoke the words of the *kiddush* softly as her hands moved gracefully well above the lighted candelabra. All eyes were on her until Lutz intoned a haunting song in Hebrew. As the melody faded, he closed his eyes. Next, all took part in drinking the first cup of wine. *This is reminiscent of holy communion,* Lenny thought. Then, at Deborah's insistence, Lenny rose from his chair and walked the hand-washing basin to all participants. Small hand towels were provided to each guest for drying their hands.

Then Lutz asked each guest to take a sprig of parsley and dip it in saltwater, the green representing the hopefulness of spring and the saltwater the tears of slavery. As he gave the explanation, there was the sheen of sadness in many eyes.

Aunt Sofia spoke with sorrow in her voice. "Let us all remember our loved ones in Ukraine who are facing enslavement at this very moment. I never thought I would have to pray for freedom and release of my former neighbors at this stage of my life." She touched Lutz's hand and smiled at him. He read the sorrow flooding her eyes.

All bowed their heads as Lutz started to pray. "Almighty, be with all who are in danger and threatened to lose all they have. More urgently, heed our prayers for their safety and well-being. Guide those fleeing to safety, and be on the side of the men defending their country. Bring an end to this war and give us peace." All nodded in consensus.

Then, Lutz walked the participants through the fifteen stages of the Pesach Seder with sincerity and devotion to his faith, stopping to partake of the meal and drinking of wine appropriate to the stage within the ceremony. When they reached *Hallel,* they drank the fourth cup of wine and joined in a song of praise. Finally, *Nirtzah* marked the end of the ritual, and Lutz and Deborah spoke in unison *"L'shanah haba'a b'irushalayim!"* which means, "Next year in Jerusalem!" All were wondering where they might be during Passover 2023.

Staff from *Die Kurve* cleared the table and helped arrange chairs to provide excellent viewing of the presentation Lenny had prepared.

Maksym turned to Aunt Sofia. "I wonder what is yet to come?"

She raised her shoulders repeatedly. Joy and sadness alike filled her eyes. "Just wait and see. You might discover things you couldn't imagine in your wildest dreams." She smiled at her boy.

Is she losing it? He wondered.

Deborah dimmed the lights as Lenny couldn't wait to start the program. As the first image appeared on the screen, a slightly faded video began showing a slender woman bent over a twin crib. However, it wasn't the image that commanded everyone's immediate attention. It was the eerie sound of a clarion alto voice singing *Abendsegen* from Engelbert Humperdinck's opera "Hänsel und Gretel."

Maksym stared at his brother. It was an awakening from a dream that took him back to long-forgotten times. *"Wie aus der Ferne längst vergang'ner Zeiten"* [as from the distance of long-forgotten times] from Wagner's *Fliegender Holländer* came to his mind. He spoke at last. "I remember the song. I remember the voice. It was often sung to us by a woman. Who is that woman and where is she?"

Lutz needed to control his voice. He was fearful it would break in mid-sentence. "The woman in this video is Señora Doretta García López. This video was filmed by her husband Señor Fernando García López in the García López hacienda in the Maipo Valley near Santiago, Chile. The original was a Kodak movie produced in December 1968. The twins to whom the woman is singing were Elijah Avraham and Eduardo Emmanuel García López. They are our nephews."

"Can we see more? I'm intrigued," Matviyko said.

There were numerous slides of the twins as they changed from babies to toddlers and eventually to energetic boys aged three. They were often held by the slender woman and the man called Fernando. The following slide was of an older woman. She stood next to the boys as she leaned on an elegantly fashioned cane heavily encrusted with silver and turquoise.

Maksym squinted. "Could you zoom in on that image? The hairstyle, posture, and cane got my attention. She looks familiar. I've seen her before. But she spoke a different language. What was her name?"

"Her name was Señora Esmeralda García López. She was Fernando's mother; that is, she was Elijah and Eduardo's grandmother. Señora Esmeralda was of noble birth and was a force to be reckoned with."

The following slide was that of a large dog. Matviyko's eyes became as large as saucers. "Pablo! That is Pablo!" he shouted.

"Are you sure that was the dog's name? I thought they called him 'Fritzchen' or something like that," Lutz said.

"Don't try to confuse me. That dog was Pablo," Matviyko said with conviction in his voice.

"My brother is right. That dog's name was Pablo," Maksym spoke. "How he loved charging around in the labyrinth. You can see it right there in the background."

Lenny moved along with the slideshow. Another short video clip showed Fernando speaking with a young woman, Juanita, as they were walking along the road with a pram holding both boys. Mario apparently had been doing the filming.

Maksym asked for the clip to be repeated. "I know that voice. Who is it?"

Lenny spoke "It's the voice of the boys' father. He's instructing the nursemaid working for the family."

"I swear I've heard that voice before," Matviyko said.

"Do you have another photo of the woman who sang that song in the opening video? Unfortunately, I couldn't really tell how she looked because she was shown in profile," Maksym asked.

An outcry brought the presentation to a sudden halt. It was Nataliya wailing in pain. "Anton, Anton. It's time for me to be rushed to the hospital. My water just broke. Forgive me, Herr Osram. I didn't mean to spoil your evening, much less ruin your beautiful Asian rug."

"Don't you worry about a thing," Lenny said.

Anton reached for his wife with the assistance of her father, Maksym. Daryna couldn't help herself. There were tears of joy rather than those of sadness. All the others looked on in silence. Nataliya yelped again. "I feel the baby coming. I don't believe there's enough time to have me hospitalized."

Lenny sprung into action. "Lutz, take her to my bedroom. Thank God Frau Nötig put fresh linens on the bed. Nothing worth fretting about. Anna and I never expected hearing a newborn's outcry in our bedroom. How she would have loved this moment." His eyes reflected the joy he was allowed to experience.

Deborah rushed to the kitchen, locating the largest vessel she could find. Only minutes later she succeeded in having a kettle with warm water to wash the newborn and birth mother. Warm compresses helped the woman in labor as well.

Matviyko asked for an apron. None was to be found. Lutz grabbed a terrycloth towel and fastened it around Matviyko's slender waist.

Anton desperately tried to reach Dr. Braun, Nataliya's ob/gyn. At last, Dr. Braun returned the call and tried to put Anton at ease. "Is she bedded down and stripped of unnecessary garments? If so, let me see her condition using your phone. Then, I'll talk you through it."

Anton could see the crown of the baby's head emerging. He nearly passed out at the sight of the bloody-appearing fluid surrounding the baby's head. "I can't do this."

"Yes, you can, and you will."

"Her uncle, Dr. Matviyko, has to do it. He's ready. I'll help Nataliya with her breathing efforts."

Matviyko positioned himself under cover of a sheet and faced Nataliya's exposed body. "One more good push, Nataliya," he yelled, extending his hand to receive the baby emerging quickly. An exuberant outburst announced the arrival of a healthy baby boy. "Now, that wasn't so difficult, was it?" he said.

Dr. Braun was about to comment when Matviyko held the phone close to Nataliya's vagina.

"I believe we are in for a surprise. Nothing to worry about."

All who were present in Lenny's bedroom were stunned into silence.

Dr. Braun acted like the coolest cat in town. "Just lay number one on mom's breast and have her assist number two with another firm push."

"You must be kidding," Anton said.

"No, I'm not. Remember you and Nataliya didn't want to know any details. I was sworn to keep my mouth shut. You are about to become the father of twins. It shouldn't really shock you. The possibility was always on the horizon. Nataliya's father is a twin. As I said, Nataliya did it once and knows the drill."

No sooner had everyone swallowed hard, digesting Dr. Braun's proclamation and instructions, when the crown of the twin emerged. Matviyko couldn't believe his eyes when he beheld the body of a baby girl who announced her arrival with a healthy outcry, not to be outdone by her ten-minute older brother.

Dr. Braun congratulated Nataliya and Anton and the delivery crew. "I'm in my car and halfway there. Just lay the babies on their mommy's tummy and cover them with a clean sheet or blanket. I'll be there in about twenty minutes and do the rest. Nothing to worry about."

That's easy to say for you, ran through Anton and Nataliya's minds.

Deborah had warmed soft blankets and gently covered the newborns' bodies now comfortably breathing as they lay on their mother's abdomen.

Nataliya wasn't bothered by the moist feel of the babies' skin as she ran her hand across their backs, joy flooding her eyes as she sensed the warmth of their soft bodies clinging to hers. "Now, what shall we name them? We had not expected a boy." She laid her hand on the baby girl's head. "You are easy. We planned to name you Henrietta Sofia," she smiled at Anton.

"We don't need to make that decision now," Anton said.

They heard the car door slam, and Lenny moved quickly to let Dr. Braun into the house. "Come in, come in. This was an unexpected pleasure. Not in my wildest dreams could I have imagined hearing the first cries of two newborns in this old house. All is okay. The uncle did a fine job delivering the babies with your help. Modern technology is a wonder."

Dr. Braun, a relatively young man, rushed ahead of Lenny. With his little black bag in hand, he followed the sound of several people talking to find mother and children safely ensconced in Lenny's bedroom. He asked all to return to the living room except Deborah and Anton.

Anton looked into Nataliya's eyes, not wanting to watch as the doctor cut the cords and freed the mother of the placentas. Deborah acted as efficiently as any trained nurse in handing Dr. Brown any instruments he needed.

Deborah breathed easily after the babies were properly washed and now wrapped in clean and warm blankets. There were no clothes at hand. *Even Christ was just wrapped in a swaddling cloth,* she thought.

The babies held against Nataliya's breasts, began to suckle and all was well. Dr. Braun assured her he would check in on her in the morning. However, he thought it was best for the mother and babies not to be moved until later the next day. "I'm sure your host won't mind overnighting in his guest quarters," he winked at Lenny.

"Right you are. I probably will be just as comfortable in my lounger after I've toasted this event a few times." He walked the doctor to the front door.

Maksym and Daryna sneaked Aunt Sofia into Lenny's bedroom

when they saw Lenny accompany Dr. Braun to the front door. The proud grandparents and the old aunt beheld the little family with awe. Aunt Sofia's hand reached out, wanting to touch the crowns of dark hair covering the babies' heads, her face reflecting nothing but joy. Maksym couldn't help hugging Daryna as he was moved by the sight of their first grandchildren.

"Who would have ever thought they would be born on this night? Never mind they. We expected only one. I guess I'm still in shock. I'm so glad Matviyko wasn't fazed at all by the challenge. I'm not sure I could've done it," Maksym admitted.

"Yes, you could have if no one else had been there to do it." Daryna smiled at her husband with pride.

Anton joined the others in the dining room after Nataliya and the babies rested comfortably.

"I need a drink."

Lenny popped the first bottle of German sparkling wine as all gathered again around the large table. "We must toast the successful new arrivals before we finish the evening."

Varida kept talking about how much easier things would've been if Ivan had been present for the event. Walter thought sparkling wine was the last thing she needed, but he knew how to choose his battles. He loved her dearly, but sometimes her friend in the bottle annoyed him—not only annoyed but concerned him. *Next time I talk with Ivan, I'll bring it to his attention. Maybe he can talk some sense into Varida.*

All eyes were once again on Lenny. "I've forgotten what you asked me, Maksym, before we shifted gears. Do you recall?" He mumbled something about his eighty-nine-year-old failing memory.

"I do. Of course I do. How could I forget? I wanted to see a better image of the woman who was seen in that opening video."

"That's right. Now I remember." Lenny flipped through the program and found a close-up of Doretta. When he projected it onto the screen, Maksym and Matviyko held their breaths.

"When you opened the program, who did you say she was?" they asked in one voice.

"The woman is Señora Doretta Osram García López. She was our sister. And yes, she was your mother who loved you very much. So when you were taken from your family in 1971, it broke her heart." Wetness was streaming down Lutz's face. Lenny couldn't hide his sadness as he recalled the day.

There were tears in everyone's eyes.

Aunt Sofia hugged Maksym and smiled across the table at Matviyko. "You've been found. You are safe once again with your family. From the moment I learned that you were stolen from your loved ones, I prayed every day for this moment. God listened to me." She reached into her left sleeve for a lace handkerchief and dabbed her eyes.

Maksym's eyes focused on Lutz. "What made you even think that we could be Elijah and Eduardo?"

"It's all Lenny's fault. He spotted you sitting at the bar *Im Goldenen Kessel* on that night in early February and was stunned by our uncanny resemblance. He thought he was looking at the two of us when we were forty years younger. It was fate. When he read your mother's letter she sent to your great-grandmother the day you were born, we knew what to look for."

The following was a closeup of Maksym, highlighting the birthmark on his cheek. "When I hugged you after you shaved off that damn beard, I knew who you were. Unfortunately for you, I didn't have the heart to tell you and spoil the party. You could have saved yourself the two-hundred euro you spent on DNA testing. The agency missed the boat by not getting the results back to us in time. I don't give a damn what they find and tell us. You're part and parcel of the tribe." Lutz winked at Lenny and his nephews.

"He's right!" Lenny concurred.

Maksym regained his composure. "Tell us about the lady with the fancy cane."

"She was your grandmother, indeed. Grandmother Esmeralda nearly lost her mind when you were stolen at the Hacienda while your family was on that trip to Antarctica. She felt responsible for you and sent a wire to the captain of the ship. When your family was informed of the devastating news of your disappearance when their ship arrived in Ushuaia, they rushed to their plane. Your father was so shaken that he nearly crashed when they flew back to Santiago. The servants cautioned your father when he returned to the hacienda. Your grandmother hid in her bedroom. He thought he was looking at Mrs. Havisham in Dicken's *Great Expectations. The Madwoman of Chaillot* entered his mind. Grandmother Esmeralda was dressed in her wedding gown which she'd torn to shreds. Her hair hung around her face, tangled and in a mess. He was certain she'd gone insane." Lutz took a deep breath. "But it wasn't anyone in the family's fault," he said.

"What was the fate of our family in Chile?" Maksym then asked.

"No one knows what happened to your parents and your older brother, Mario, and your sister, Alona. They were abducted on September 11, 1973, by marauders who were affiliated with General Augusto Pinochet. Your loved ones became victims of the Chilean coup d'état ousting the Allende regime," Lutz stated. "Your parents belonged to the upper crust in Chilean society and were targeted by the criminals. The bandits annihilated anyone with opposing political views. It's not unlike what's going on right now."

Lenny spoke. "Supposedly your family was taken to the torture ship *La Esmeralda* which was moored in Valparaiso. Hundreds of Pinochet's victims were tortured to death and disposed of at sea. By a strange coincidence, the torture vessel bore the name of your Chilean grandmother." Lenny beheld his nephews and wiped his eyes with his hand.

Maksym reached across the table wanting to touch his brother's hand. "We never knew we had a brother and sister; at least we never recalled them after we were taken. So how do you know what really happened to our family? Are you just speculating?"

"Your mother's maid had a German friend in Santiago who contacted your German grandmother with the sad news. Our mother had met her during visits to Santiago," Lenny said.

Lutz spoke then. "The hoodlums burned the Garcia López Hacienda to the ground. Loyal servants found your grandmother the following day. Pablo, your trusted dog, led them to the wooden shed where the wings for the Wind Angels were stored. They found her hanging between the gently moving angelic appendages. The sign hanging from her neck read "*Perra*" meaning "Bitch or Slut." They were hateful humans who didn't deserve to walk this earth."

"Who are the Wind Angels?" Maksym wanted to know.

"Your brother, Mario, filmed them in action when your German grandmother and her second husband visited your family after your disappearance. It was a rare occasion for the Wind Angels to perform."

Lenny found Mario's video and played it for all to see. There was total silence among the Seder celebrants as they listened to Doretta's haunting voice and the Wind Angels humming the *Abendsegen.* "The women walked between kerosene torches, spreading the warmth the heaters generated unto the grapes with the wing-like appendages attached to their arms. It was the Wind Angels and their movements who saved the grape harvest from falling victim to the sudden chill descending from the Andes mountains," Lenny said.

Peeking out the large windows of Lenny's house, they spotted the almost full moon barely hinting at its waxing stage. Some stars were much brighter than others. Lutz couldn't help himself. He thought of Bette Davis's last line in "Now Voyager"—*Don't let's ask for the moon, we have the stars!* Just then Lenny touched the button for the last image to be cast on the screen. It was a photo of their father, Fernando, standing beside an unknown male figure. Fernando was tall and slender; the man close to him was over-towering. Actually gigantic—crowned by an enormous head.

Aunt Sofia gasped, calling attention to the stranger, vehemently pointing at the image. Her outcry frightened Varida and Daryna. All eyes were on Aunt Sofia as she stared at the projection on the oversized screen. She had pressed the linen napkin against her open mouth to stifle her sobbing.

"Who is that man?" Matviyko asked. There was anger and fright in his voice.

"It's the Giant Shadow," Maksym blurted. "It's the guy who gave me nightmares for all these years." He'd risen from his chair to look closer at the projected image.

Aunt Sofia's eyes were fixed on what she saw. "Oh, my God! You're right. He's the one who dumped the two of you on the floor in the house in Yalta. It was he who made a deal with Satan. And it was he who demanded the money Popov had promised him." Everyone stared at Aunt Sofia.

Lenny looked at the slide. Mario had titled it: "Dad and Walter Hague, Flight Instructor." Then, puzzled, he cast his eyes on Maksym and Matviyko.

"Bastard!" Lenny said. "He knew your parents were away. Walter Hague also was aware that there was much wealth to be had. Hague had arranged the purchase of the plane your father bought. It involved close to one million dollars. He might have thought of collecting a huge ransom and changed his mind. On the other hand, he might have been in cahoots with the forces planning the coup d'état for Pinochet two years later. Who knows? And he had his own plane." Lenny caught his breath.

Miserable prick," Lutz spat.

Maksym stood up and walked over to Lutz. He extended his arms, wanting to hug the man. "I'm so sorry I never got to know my mother, your dear sister. I can still hear her voice in my head. I will never hear the *Abendsegen* again and not have that image of my mother before me. Thank you for finding us. Thank you for bringing us home." He sobbed on Lutz's shoulder.

Matviyko was overcome by what he saw and heard. "The party is over." He never dealt well with emotional scenes.

"No. It's just beginning. You were lost and now you are found. Call it what you may: Serendipity, *Kismet, Schicksal,* divine intervention, *Karma,* chance, fate, predestination, destiny, fortune, providence, or whatever. It brought us together on that fateful night at *Im Goldenen Kessel.* Deep in our guts, Lutz and I knew who you were," Lenny said.

"Welcome to our world, Elijah Avraham García López Maksym Popov and Eduardo Emmanuel García López Matviyko Popov." Lutz beamed. "When asked about the length of your names, you'll have much explaining to do. I believe you'll be able to do it," he added. "You may call me Uncle Lutz. I've never had the honor to be called an uncle."

Anton smiled and looked at Maksym, his father-in-law. "Our big surprise, our little boy, just found his name. He shall be called Anton Avraham Emmanuel."

Acknowledgments

It gives me great pleasure to see another of my novels reach the stage of publication. I'm especially thankful for a small group of dedicated readers and their many comments, suggestions, and corrections. This circle of friends includes, Kevin Burns, Eric Hucke, Bette Packer, Duke Southard, and Vikki Stea. Special thanks go to Joan E. Angevine for her thoughtful review and comments pertaining to Resurrection. My sincere gratitude goes to the staff of Wheatmark Publishing for their efforts in bringing this latest novel to fruition. I wish to recognize especially Wheatmark's Senior Project Manager, Lori Conser, for her dedicated and diligent work leading to the publication of my writings during the past seven years. Many thanks are due those who have encouraged me to continue writing, especially the members of the Green Valley Writers' Forum and family and friends. Last but not least, I want to extend my appreciation to my wife, Lynne, with heartfelt thankfulness for her endless hours of reading and providing suggestions during the creative process, critical editorial commentary, and invaluable support throughout my many hours of writing. Thanks, Lynne, for your loyal support for fifty-nine years.

THE HOUSE ON ROSALINDENSTRAßE

Preview

Harald Lutz Bruckner

Prologue

DREAMS can take us into a world that excites us immensely or frightens us to the core. Last night's nocturnal adventure afforded me a glance back at an old house I had known since I was a small boy.

Moving about, I was surrounded by a thick pea soup London fog. The whole thing was absurd—and yet real. Passing storm clouds drifted eastward in a lazy mood, leaving an almost full moon to cast eerie shadows on the handsome building known as Rosalindenstraße 36. It was built at the turn of the last century and withstood the vagaries of time and two world wars. Its occupants suffered through inflation of unheard proportions, times of depression, hunger, deprivation, and the highs and lows of their lives. Were it capable of speaking, the dwelling would share the tales of the rise and fall of a dynasty.

In a flash I was taken back seventy-three years. Grandmother was lying in their bedroom, located in the third of the old house totally destroyed during the last bomb attack on March 11, 1945. Miraculously it was restored. In my nocturnal wanderings I was in the presence of my dying Grandmother. Mom, her youngest sister, and I were the only witnesses, watching the last minutes of Grandma's life. The old matriarch didn't fade away quietly; she fought back to the bitter end. With her dying breath she pleaded with her youngest daughter to assure her she'd say the Lord's prayer just once in her life. The promise never passed the young woman's lips. My mother gently touched Grandmother's eyelids and closed them forever. She said prayers for her mother's departed soul. Grandmother remained the only person who died before my eyes for the next forty-one years.

Rosalindenstraße 36 was never my home, but it was where my ancestors conducted business, lived, birthed, and raised their families, and died. As I stepped into the entryway, the smells of blood, strong detergents, wet wool, and strange odors hung in the air. Steam escaped from the *Wurstküche* [sausage kitchen] and fogged my glasses. I peeked into the breakfast nook adjacent to the butcher shop where a huge round oak table surrounded by eight sturdy unoccupied chairs stood before me. I glared at Grandfather's mammoth safe. None of the piles of gold coins amassed before the outbreak of World War I were in evidence. I remembered the telling of the story. How often did Mother relive those days? Three oversized laundry baskets, now empty, stood to the side. They were filled mainly with gigantic paper bills that amounted to worthless trillions in the early 1920s. On Grandfather's daily journeys to the slaughter-houses, thousands of bills bought next to nothing. Had I been around, I would have read the desperation in all their eyes. Now I envisioned the ghostly remains of their faces. *What might they look like after being buried for decades? Morbid thoughts.* Turning away from those long-ago memories, I passed doors leading to other rooms on the ground floor.

One led to the tiniest apartment. Another to the necessary room reputedly the venue of humorous adventures. I recall my mother telling one of the stories. Grandpa needed to use the tiny WC in response to an emergency call from Mother Nature and failed to lock the door, worse yet, not even close it. Then, he heard the footfall of another needy person and didn't trust his eyes as he peered over the top of his glasses. The naked behind of his sister-in-law was about to wind up in his lap. Seeing the door open and in great need of relieving herself, she had pulled down her pants in anticipation of a quick landing, not realizing that Grandpa occupied the seat. It was his frightful scream that stopped Aunt Mimi in her tracks. I don't know how often we laughed out loud when hearing the funny tale.

Grasping the banister, I ascended to the second level and halted for a moment to catch my breath. My grandparents used to live there. In my mind's eye, I saw the old man hobbling about on crutches as he returned from having used the WC across from the living room. Throwing the helpful devices to the floor with a curse, he'd plop himself with his soiled pants into his favorite chair. Closing my eyes for a moment, I decided to climb further and start my exploration on the fifth floor. Struggling with my breathing, I had to stop at each level. I wondered how the maids carrying laundry baskets filled with damp clothes ever did it. No matter how well mangled by the hand wringer, the weight of those baskets must have been a challenge, and the women had to be clearly well-endowed with strength and adrenalin. I pushed open the door to the attic—obviously no longer locked.

I faced an empty and chilling vastness. The moonlight penetrating narrow windows created an eeriness that frightened me. All I could see were dragging clotheslines and a threadbare rag bag with dusty clothespins. I ran my right hand across the empty strings. Aging dust left smudged lines on my sweaty palm's flesh. A careless caretaker must have left one of the windows ajar. I felt the slight movement of air. The musty smell that had permeated the lowest levels of the stairwell was replaced by cooler air that hinted at clean laundry hung there in the distant past. The total emptiness of the place reminded me of my mother's annual pronouncement that no laundry be done or hung in the attic between Christmas and Epiphany. Having violated this edict of superstition would have brought bad luck to any occupant of the dwelling during the new year. Nowadays, of course, modern washing machines and clothes driers in all of the apartments of the house rendered the need for using the attic obsolete.

I shuddered, pulled the door shut, and descended to the lower levels. Grandfather had told me once that when he ran the business, men and women working for him in the butcher shop had no choice but to live under his roof. They were housed on the upper floors. He enjoyed knowing where those who labored for him lived. This way he had complete control over their comings and goings. It spoke to Grandfather's need to manipulate the lives of those who surrounded him.

Mother often described the Sunday morning procedure. Everyone under her father's roof had to attend church. Grandpa would inspect the premises and wipe everything that could hide a hint of grease or dirt with a sparkling white cloth. The wrath of God came down on those responsible for such neglect. All lined up in the courtyard like organ pipes and were handed their pay for the week. Offenders of the clean cloth were not rewarded until their sin had been exorcised.

Holding firmly onto the banister, I tackled the steep stairway. My feet halted at the door opened by my grandmother. My grandfather never came to greet me; for most of his later life, he was crippled by arthritis.

I passed the music room, where the old upright piano was covered with grime. I glanced at the yellowed sheet music standing lopsided on the old ivory easel resting on the piano. It bore the title "Overtüre Orpheus in der Unterwelt" by Jacques Offenbach. Then I recalled my mother sitting there and playing this favorite of hers. No way could I get that melody out of my head. My mind was bewitched by the echoing sound.

Backing slowly out of the room, I continued down the long hallway toward the last room. The metal heel plates on my leather-soled shoes made noises that bounced off the walls down the narrow passage. Smells of cinnamon hung in the air as I crossed the kitchen. At last, I arrived at the furthest room, my grandparents' sleeping quarters. I pressed down the brass handle on the bedroom door and hesitantly pushed my way into the room. I stared at the empty bed crafted from heavy white oak; its sheen dull with time. The smell of death seemed to hang in the air.

I turned back, and my feet carried me once again past the living room. I glanced into the well-known space. Grandpa's urine-stained overstuffed chair now stood empty. More than six decades had passed since the man who conceived erecting the house on Rosalindenstraße found eternal sleep at the Parkfriedhof. Now I felt the angst of being whipped with a willow cane and read the pleasure in Grandfather's eyes as he inflicted pain on me—a young boy. I could feel the hurt on my buttocks. Then I recalled the old man sitting in front of his wall safe, listening to his greedy daughters as they fought over the spoils after their mother had been buried. I felt as if I was viewing once again a scene from King Lear.

I woke up bathed in perspiration. My sleepwalk through the old house made me sad. Now fully awake, reality transported me back to another night. Deep in my psyche was an event that happened in 1996 and forever changed the house's history on Rosalindenstraße.

About the Author

Harald Lutz Bruckner, author of *The Blue Sapphire Amulet, Escape on the Astral Express, A Wanderer on the Earth, The Born-Again Phoenix, Harald's Garland, Lighthouse Mystery, Doretta's Damnation, A Backward Glance at Eden, Obsessive Compulsion, and Forever Greta* hails from Germany but has spent his adult life in the United States. His work and educational adventures have taken him from merchandising/retailing, the teaching of German and World Literature, to a career in Audiology and the challenges of working with hard-of-hearing and deaf children and adults. Among his favorite academic subjects to teach were his offerings in sign language. In 1981, he discovered the magic of painting in transparent watercolors and has never stopped painting. Moving to sunny Arizona from the High Country of Colorado in 2003, caused a major shift in his subject matter, changing from a primarily realistic orientation to one of total abstraction. Since his retirement from Academia, Bruckner pursued his passions for travel, art, music, and the enjoyment of writing.